Vi⸻ natu⸻ a scr⸻ bag.

"I'm goin, ⸻

"I heard you, Victoria. Goodbye."

God please leave don't make it ugly it's been so beautiful the most beautiful time. Even the stupid parts have been beautiful, let's just be incompatible, not ugly. Please.

"Well? Ain't you gon say nothin else? Or are you just gonna sit up there with that lil old funny lookin beanie stuck on the back of your head'n stare at me like I'm crazy or somethin?"

David glared into Victoria's face, both of his eyes squeezed into murderous slits.

"Get out of here," he said softly, viciously.

"You don't have to be so mean and nasty about it! I was just joking about your lil old—"

"Get out of here before I kill you!"

Victoria struck another pose, placing one hand on her hip and flexed her left leg provocatively, took a close look at the malicious brightness in David's eyes and thought better of making a protest.

David wrenched the door open behind her.

"Get out now!"

She slunk past him, avoiding his eyes and, a few paces down the hall, turned, sadly.

"I didn't know you was so sensitive."

He slammed the door shut, tears clouding his vision.

Why is love so dangerous for me?

SECRET MUSIC

a book by

ODIE HAWKINS

An Original Holloway House Edition
HOLLOWAY HOUSE PUBLISHING CO.
LOS ANGELES, CALIFORNIA

Published by
HOLLOWAY HOUSE PUBLISHING COMPANY
8060 Melrose Avenue, Los Angeles, CA 90046
International Standard Book Number 0-87067-265-7
Printed in the United States of America
Cover photograph by Jeffrey
Cover design by Jeff Renfro

Dedicated to

Faye Lattimore
Ade Ogonsewe
Raymond Friday Locke

powerful people

BOOK ONE

Secret Music

Chapter 1

Alias The Great Lawd Buddha

Chester L. Simmons, alias "the Great Lawd Buddha," stood off by himself in a corner of the exercise yard, warming his cold bones in the bright autumn sun and reading a letter from his son, Chester, Jr.

He smiled at the son's description of his second grandchild, "a rubber faced brown bouncer of a baby boy."

The Great Lawd finished the letter finally, tilted his face up toward the sun, slightly slanted eyes closed, soaking in the warmth.

Life in the joint wasn't so bad, he rationalized for a moment, the sun's rays tripping him out, not if you had three squares a day, few hassles and a chance to write as much as you wanted.

He slowly lowered his head, his prison issued baseball cap

shrouding his face with shadows. No, he scratched his earlier thought, no, that's not right . . . being in jail is pure hell.

He looked out across the yard, his eyes sweeping across a panorama of misery, self hate, dumb rage, hostility, inhumane cruelty and human degradation.

Chester L. Simmons, "the Great Lawd Buddha," Mississippian, black brotherman, poet, dramatist, world spieler, artist, speculator, murderer.

His thoughts twisted away from the snake pit scene in front of him, back in time, to his life with Josie "Heatwave" Scott, the one time apple of his eye, the lady who made him blow his cool . . . six times into her gorgeous body with a German luger.

Why did it have to be Josie? Why Josie? He'd asked himself a few dozen profound times, behind a terrible day under a sadistic guard, or after a dismal night dreaming of the flavor of her body's aromas, the warmth of her eyes, the shape of her nose, her lush mouth, her neck, her gorgeous titties, her navel, her rainbow hips, the grizzled sporran between her thighs, her magnificent ass . . . thoughts that took him beyond momentary unpleasantries, like doing twenty to life.

But, life being what it is, he philosophized, it had to be Josie . . . sigghhh . . . c'est la vie.

He plunged his hands deeper into his pockets, the anguish of five thousand hours of remorse tilting his face back up into the sun, seeking warmth, oblivion from haunted memories. They were on him before he was aware of their presence.

"Whass happenin', bruh Buddha?" the boldest of the trio entre'd.

He pinned all three evenly. Tough, hip, literate young black captives, into books 'n politics. Good.

"Nothin' to it, lil' brothers, a baby could do it."

He leaned against the cement wall at his back and crossed his legs. Which one would pop the question? They alway

10

3 1833 03080 1408

had something to ask, something they wanted to know. "Buddha, what's this shit we hear 'bout you being declared a white man in South Africa?" Marcus, the bank robber asked point blank and squatted in place to hear the full story.

"Ohh, that," Buddha supercasually tossed off and squatted himself down slowly into his Sumo wrestling rest stance, glad to talk a lil' stuff to open minds.

"That ... hah hah ... that was the result of a most weird set of circumstances, most weird. If I could possibly bum a cigarette from one of you golden brothers, I would be most happy to run the whole thing down to you."

Marcus held his pack out to him immediately, pleased to be able to supply the bribe.

One could never tell, one day, it might be candy, one day a lil' powdered nutmeg to snort, or snuff or cocaine, but most often, just a few cigarettes.

"It all started after I had to make my European break, behind my heroin sting. I told you all about that, didn't I? Being hounded by those Algerian mafia dudes over that kilo I copped?"

The three men nodded solemnly, one of their favorite dramas. "O.K., there I was, once again, on a freighter ... I used to go a lotta places on freighters, this time as a common swabbie. I had stolen or traded for a Malay seaman's documents who looked like me, on the way to wherever the brute that I was treadin' water on, was headed.

Now, why we had to wind up in Capetown, South Africa is something that only God above and the captain of the sleazy bitch we was sailin' on could answer. Cape-town, South Africa," he enunciated syllable by syllable, as though grinding his teeth on something bitter.

"I'll never know why, what demonic force caused me to jump ship in a place like that, but I did. In many ways it was, unequivocally, one of the grooviest black places I've ever been

11

in this world. I mean, like sho' nuff groovy gut bucket black. Everybody after white, that is to say, the so called colored, Cape Malays, Indians, Zulus, Xosas, Basutos, Pondos, everybody but white helped everybody else.

"I had some dudes help put together all the documents I needed, just to walk the streets. Them crazy Boers had one of the most insane pass systems the world has ever seen, put together by one of our country's great computer companies. Dig it?

"I had people feed me, and lawd knows they didn't have much, pass me around like I was a cookie that might crumble up in their hands," his voice rumbled dramatically, "because I was a soul brother from the United States who had decided, they thought, to stay with them in their locations, share their oppression and their fight for liberation. Beautiful people, gentlemen, beautiful people, carved out of love."

He accepted another cigarette, chain fashion, and carried on, caught up by his story.

"I had three families slip me around in their location for two weeks, just ahead of the state police—the Gestapo is really what they were. Now dig it! I feel I must elaborate on this point because it is most important. I was a potentially dangerous, slick minded United States nigger who had obviously jumped ship for subversive reasons, and was known to do my share of dirt ... that is, if the whole truth be known."

Donnell, Marcus and Brian all held their hands out to be slapped, their common sense of wrong doing embroidered for them in a way that they had never heard it before.

"The South African police, brothermen," he continued more slowly, in a heavier tone, "the South African police could bring pee to a chump's eyes, if they caught you gettin' down wrong, missin' a step, or doin' any such shit as they could misconstrue being against their regime.

"And there I was, young, foolish, wild, so crazy that I didn't

12

even know why I had jumped ship. Well, the rats, no women and lousy food may have been contributing factors.

"Some of the militant brothers thought I had come over secretly as a black Che Guevara, but actually, that wasn't it at all.

"It was just stupidity what done it. Nobody had ever really told me about the racial set up, really. Nobody had told me that the Afrikkaners discriminated against everybody, even they own mommas."

The trio laughed indulgently, pulling their collars up against the deepening chill.

"Yeahhh, that's right! Even they own mommas! There was a case while I was there, of a police inspector who caught his momma with the yardboy and was so outraged that he had the Racial Classification Board declare his momma one piece nigger, shifted her away from him, had the Re-Classification Board bypass him and kept on livin' happily ever after with his snow white wife. Helluva country, gentlemen! I'm tellin' ya the nachul bone truth! Helluva country!"

Marcus nodded in serious agreement, his reading having covered the South African Cancer.

"After a bit, some of the dudes who were looking out for me, at the risk of their lives, helped me get a gig . . . underground, down in the diamond mines."

"Diamond mines?!" Donnell showed the gold caps on his teeth in surprise.

"That's what you heard, amigo . . . diamonds! Diamonds!" The Great Lawd Buddha licked his lips and sparkled his eyes in the oblique rays of the setting sun, caricaturing greed.

"Every morning at 4:30 a.m. we slaves, yeahhh, that's just about what we were too, slaves . . . makin' so little a day, when you think about how much income we were makin' for the Baas, translated meaning Boss.

"But actually goin' deeper than that 'cause they had a system based on that Baas thing called Baaskap or Baaskamf or somethin' like that, that was supposed to keep everybody unwhite, underground for the rest of their lives, and after they died, they'd get left there, underground."

Marcus jammed his hands deeper into his blue denim jacket pockets and scowled at the wall above Buddha's head.

"Sounds like Miss'ssippi, or New Yawk, don't it?"

"Really!" Donnel affirmed, quietly slapping Buddha's out-stretched hand.

"But actually it was worse than that. Much worse. At any rate, I'm down underneath the ground, siftin' diamonds up big as your fist, turning each 'n every one into the Baas, 'til one day my treacherous United States nigger mind started shootin' off sparks.

"I knew that some of the dudes managed to get away with a few tiny, industrial type gems every month. What I wanted to do was cop some authentic stones.

"So, I got on my job. It was really hard for awhile, to get my organization together. I mean, like a few of the most un-sophisticated African brothers didn't even feel that it was right to steal from the Baas."

"Buddha! You got to be jivin'!"

"I wouldn't jive you, youngblood," he answered.

"But you see, their minds were formed in a tribal mold, they didn't think it was right to steal from *anybody,* and to lots of 'em, despite the fact that they suffered under him, the white man was still a human being.

"Deep, huh? Probably one of the main reasons why all those black folks over there haven't formed a wall and just pushed the sucker into the sea. Anyway, after a bit, I escaped from the mines—"

"Escaped?" Brian exclaimed.

"Uhhh huhhnnn, e-scaped. You see, at that time, you signed a 'contract' for two years and the only way you could break it was to e-scape. I escaped and became a fence for the dudes I had organized in the mines.

"My thang went a lil' bit like this; I'd pay about 25 dollars for a helluva gem, 50, U.S. rates, for a fantastic gem and 100, at least, for one of those overwhelming pinkie rings that you sometimes see on the small fingers of eminent homos and stark ravin' rich Harlem pimps. I moved fast, bought everything that I could get my hands on, dealt with a rich ol', unscrupulous diamond merchant who had an interest in the mines that the stones were being ripped off from. He really had a number goin'. He couldn't lose for winnin' . . . makin' grand theft coins from both ends.

"You dudes ever see a diamond merchant?"

The three men mechanically nodded no in unison.

"Well, take my word for it, they, 'long with the diamond cutters, are weird lookin' lil' bitty dudes. They all got pointed heads, usually bald and don't have no emotion whatsoever and would do anything for diamonds. Love them diamonds.

"The dude I was dealin' with, tryin' to pull a super grand stake together, in order to split the scene, tried to have me arrested a couple times, and when that didn't work, I got word of what was goin' down through the grapevine, tried to have me assassinated. All he cared about was diamonds . . . period."

He stood up to stretch his legs and eased back down into position, belly hanging over his belt, Sumo style.

"Anyway, within two months or so, I had scrounged up 'bout $600,000 worth o' gems, some really good, some pretty bad, and I was ready to hat up . . . but, as lady luck would have it, the night before I got ready to split, I was leavin' a Xosa lady's crib, a really too fine sister named Christa, at 12:30 a.m. and got picked up for a pass violation . . . and that's when the doodoo hit the propeller."

Buddha paused to exchange solemn nods with six members

15

of a Chicano group to whom he had given a Third World talk to, the day before.

"Yeahhh, it sho' nuff hit the fan," he continued, "number one, the Gestapo must have spent three or four months grillin' me, tryin' to make me tell them who the Baas was, behind my organization. The more I told them that I was, the less they believed me.

"Finally, it dawned on one of those superduper crackers that I was the Baas. Now that really twisted their lil' ol' hate filled minds around.

"Me, Chester L. Simmons from Miss'ssippi, one of their sister states, had actually been the brains behind some grand theft action . . . it was too much for 'em!

"Now what they did, some beaurocrat in the Racial Determination section, was this; since it was obvious that no black man could possibly have schemed at such a level, then I must be a white man, a member of the Baasdom.

"Wowww!, talk about goin' through some changes!" Marcus burst out, eyes digging the Great Lawd.

"Changes, you say? Uhh huh, as good a word for it as you could use. What was happenin', aside from all the money I was usin' to bribe everybody and his brother with, was this.

"On the socio-political propaganda site, the authorities didn't want any kind of word to leak out, officially, about my gettin' past the diamond mine check system. Me, a black brother!

"I mean, like, after all, that would give a lot o' people big ideas. So, therefore, in that typical iron headed way they had of doin' things, they had me declared a white man. Can you git ready for that?"

"You a bad dude, Buddha," Donnell solemnly assured him.

"By this time I'd been in the slams, in solitary for about six months, but my money was workin' for me. I managed to stick coins to the Prime Minister's uncle, even . . . anything to get out.

"Now, dig it, young brothers, I'll tell you the truth, if I'm lyin' I hope God'll strike me dead."

He paused for a cigarette and a light.

"I don't know who really decided that the best thing to do was deport me, but I sho' am grateful. Aside from my bribery, they wanted to git rid of me for socio-political reasons. They didn't want a declared white man that looked kinda black, in jail creating some weird kind of martyr for the blacks, so they forced me to agree to a deportation scene, sort of a primitive plea bargainin' number.

"Well, heyyy, you can imagine how I felt. I would've agreed to anything to get out of that place, anything!"

"Right on!" Brian cued in, alert to the circumstances.

"Well, you can believe they fucked me over a lil' bit before I was finally released. One day the guard would announce that I was leavin' that evenin', then turn right around and tell me to forget about it . . . as well as your other kinds of regular torture.

"The South African white man is a stranger to most of the rest of the human race, him and the red necked Miss'ssippian.

"I don't really know what happened to them durin' the evolutionary process, but I do know this . . . a special kind of sickness settled into both of 'em hundreds of years ago and they've never been close to being healthy."

The Great Lawd Buddha pursed his lips reflectively and slowly stood, his eyes following the lazy flight of a pidgeon.

Marcus, Donnell and Brian followed the direction of his eyes.

Brian, impatiently wanting to hear the end of Buddha's story before the evening lock up, "Uhh, so they booted you out, huh?"

"In the dead of night, my friend, in the dead of night," he continued, snatching his eyes away from the pidgeon's

17

flight, "me and three other undesirable aliens. However, I could say, as a history maker, that I had had the opportunity to be a black/white man in one of the most prejudiced white places on Mother Earth, and you can believe me, that takes some doing.

"Awright, deported, hardshippin' and in Zambia, tryin' to shit out a few of these stones I'd stuffed away in my precious lil' body."

"You got away with some?"

"Clean as a whistle! They'd made me take some laxatives 'n shit, but years ago, in India . . . that's another whole story, a great Yogaman taught me how to control my bowels.

"I mean, like I once knew how to half shit, or fart at three different tonal levels and a whole bunch of other things, but you know how it is if you don't practice.

"At any rate, I was home free, a pocketful of precious stones, off to trade with the Conquerin' Lion of Judah, the King of Kings, His Imperial Lawdship, Haile Salassie himself."

"O wowwwwww."

"Yessuh! I figured that the only righteous dude I could deal with would be the Emperor of Ethiopia. I knew, if anybody had any money at all, it would be him . . . so, off I go, to Ethiopia."

The guard on the tower station above them, concerned about lengthening shadows and the intensity of their closeness, motioned them out to the center of the yard.

Marcus scowled up at the guard. "Hey, I got a lil' home brew in my cell, y'all wanna . . . ?"

"No sooner said than done!" Buddha agreed quickly, the last rays of the sun disappearing over the wall, chilling him to the bone.

The four of them made their way through the relays of contraband searchers, up to their tier.

18

Marcus ushered them into his cell as though he were receiving guests in a swank house.

"Make yourselves to home, it ain't much but it all belongs to the state."

He uncovered a potent half pint of distilled potato drippings, rubbing alcohol, iodine (for color) and the residue of several past batches and passed it to the guest of honor.

"Oowheeee!" Buddha exclaimed, squinching up his already squinched up eyes. "Goddamn! This shit is u-gly!"

Having given it his stamp of approval, he took another long swallow. The trio beamed around him.

"Go on, Buddha, you was in Ethiopia."

"Uh huh, sho' was. Got a fair 'n square deal on my gems from His Majesty, hung around Addis A Babba long enough to sock a couple crumb rushers into a few ladies and departed, ten minutes ahead of three tribes of brothers, intent on makin' me marry their sisters . . . and a red hot case of ol' fashioned plague."

Donnell spilled a little of the homebrew out of the side of his mouth.

"What knida plague?"

"The bubonic plague, young suh, the bubonic plague. The kind that they used to have in Europe that would kill off half of London, or Paris or Amsterdam. The plague plague.

"But like I said, I was off. What I was goin' to do was hit off 'round the eastern coast, shoot through the upper Suedan right quick, slice through Egypt . . . I hadn't been to Cairo yet, whip around the edge of Libya, maybe get on back into Europe from Algeria, if everything was cool.

"As it turned out, everything was love jones, 'til I got to Algeria. Somebody had put out a contract on my body.

"I don't have to tell you who, and I guess it was stupid of me to be thinkin' that the Algerians who wanted my guts wouldn't check back home every now and then.

19

"Anyway, whilst I was dodging knives, bullets, and shit being dropped from roof tops, they had started another one of those lil' ol' funny time wars they were in the habit of havin'.

"I think this one was about some dude snatchin' some other dude's woman's veil off."

"Pass it on, Donnell," Brian reminded him as he stared hypnotically into Buddha's mouth.

Buddha accepted the half empty, half pint bottle and bowed while seated, super graciously, half lit.

"I got out," he said curtly, after a quick swallow, "are we completely cigaretteless?"

Marcus lit one and handed it to him.

"Yeahhh, I got out, fled to Casablanca, Morocco. Now that's a town for you if ever there was one! At the time I swooped in, everything went! You hear me, lil' brothers? Everything!

"I hadn't been in town fifteen hot minutes, black in white, white on black, moppin' my face with a snow white handkerchief, when two of the most beautiful lil' girls, teenagers actually . . . grabbed me to lead me to their virgin mother."

The men winked across the booze and their male feelings for those scenes.

"What could I say? What could I do? I married all three of 'em that weekend and settled down to a harmonious domestic life. I must hasten to add, right in through here, however, the kind of domestic life I had wasn't all that domestic.

"Within three months I had gotten my pinky finger into the hash trade, had my big toe into the cocaine thing, and was handlin' a few choice gems.

"I had learned a whole lot about how to judge a stone from the ol' pointy headed diamond merchant, and the rest of me was pushed off into them French diplomat's wives . . . those that had a lil' somethin' to add to the family treasury.

"But, as usual, I got greedy. The more I had, the more I wanted. I tried to corner the hash market and the king got pissed off and kicked me out. He was usin' my hash thang as an excuse, what he really wanted was my woman, Fatima."

The Great Lawd Buddha uncoiled himself slowly from Marcus' bunk, stood looking through the barred Gothic window, remembering.

When he spoke again, after long, moments of deep thought, his voice, a soundtrack of his experiences in life, carried the flavor of the *souk,* the yearning cry of the *kif fiend,* the smoke and intrigue of Northern Africa.

"Fatima . . . Fatima," he pronounced her name reverently, as though whispering into the Prophet's ear. "So beautiful, so deep and arrogant that when she walked through the streets, pin striped tattoo blued from her chin to her bottom lip, body shaped like a lovely coca cola bottle, dudes used to walk into the sides of buildings, or start prayin', right on the spot. And Aissa and Naima were just about as fine as their mother.

"So much of what was happenin' to me in those days was so mysterious, so unbelievable. Like Fatima and her daughters, for example.

"And I had to leave it all," he said suddenly, turning away from the window to remount the seat of honor.

"Yep, once again I had to leave it or run the risk of being drowned by the king's men in a sand dune somewhere."

"Hey Marcus! You got any black shoe polish?" a fellow con leaned into the cell door.

Marcus frowned, nodded no and tried to wave him away, but the brother, peeking in, caught up by the expressions on everyone's face, eased in and squatted at the foot of Marcus' bunk.

Buddha, Algerian Flamenco, wavy blue sand, homebrew, Rabat, Marrakesh, Casablanca and Fatima sizzling through his imagination, merely nodded at the addition and rapped on.

21

"After my expulsion, I don't know what happened to me, I became a lost man. It was as though my senses didn't work anymore, as though too much had happened. It was terrible, purely and simply terrible, my brothers.

"I became a souless, ash-splattered, piss-stained, dodo-covered representative of humanity, sleeping wherever my head found itself, eatin' goat turds and rat shit, searchin' for my Self again."

The addition to the group looked from one face to the other, seeking some explanation for where they were, but receiving none, listened harder.

"If you can get into what my trip was. Here, I had been declared a white man in South Africa, managed to avoid the perils of being lynched, had made it around the eastern fringe of momma Africa and all of a sudden, for only reasons that the Great It has an explanation for, I find myself in rags, walkin' down through Mauritania, tryin' my goddamnest to get to someplace on the west coast, to get on a freighter, or a slave ship, or somethin', headed for the Indies, at least. My luck had run out and I knew it."

He turned the bottle up and sipped delicately, as though it were his by reason of possession. No one bothered to correct him.

"I still had a diamond big enough to constipate an elephant in my rags, but I was savin' that for the finale, for my grand exit from Africa. What I had in mind to do was drop it in the Atlantic, a hardened tear for the souls of all our brothers 'n sisters who had jumped, been pushed, or had in some way wound up being shark's grub for a few hundred years . . . durin' the black human being trade."

Marcus, an Our-storian, looked at the Great Lawd Buddha with a tearful gleam in his eye, the homebrew almost pushing it out.

"In Africa, amongst the religious people, you always pour

22

what they call a libation to the Great It, on every occasion. That's what I had planned to do. But, as usual, Miss Fate spread her tricky fingers all over my plans.

"I wouldn't even attempt to try to take you dudes through all the supernatural trips, all the days and nights of starvation, both physical and spiritual, the times I was lost amongst people who thought I was a god, or a dog, all of the moments of intense ecstasy and profound sadness I experienced durin' my two year walk."

"Two year walk?!" the newcomer exclaimed.

"Shut up, Amos," Brian said quietly.

"Yeahhh, two years I walked," Buddha favored him with a wise, hip, old glance, "from the outskirts of Casablanca, through what they used to call the Spanish Sahara, Mauritania, Senegal, Guinea, Liberia, the Ivory Coast, on into Ghana.

"Now strangely enough, for some reason, by the time I made it to Ghana, my mind seemed to clear itself, to come alive again. All of a sudden it seemed that I was amongst my people. Can y'all get into where I'm comin' from?"

His audience nodded yes, yes, yes, yes.

"I don't know what it was, really. Maybe it was that cup of twenty-five day old palm wine a sister on the fringes of Accra laid on me, or the words of an American blood who spoke to me, or whatever, but one thing was certain, I was back in the world.

"Naturally, I wound up dealin' with the slickest motherfuckers in six countries for this stone I had. Got a decent price for it too, went out and copped some hip kente cloth robes, partied a lil' bit and the next thing I know, the Asantehene of the Ashanti people is requestin' the pleasure of my appearance.

"The Asantehene! If y'all don't know who he is, I can't begin to tell you. All I can say is this! When the Asantehene

23

wants you, you wind up being where he wants you. He's sort of like part God and part African.

"So there I am, in a huge room with the Asantehene and his linguist, that's the dude who does all his rappin' for him.

"The Asantehene is sitting on a golden throne, with gold strands of thread hangin' down over his face, a couple gold nuggets weighin' his fingers down, gold woven all into his robes. Gold, dammit! Everywhere! And the linguist, a hip lil' ol' brother about sixteen years older than kola nuts is rappin' to me, tellin' me that the Asantehene wants me to find the Golden Stool for him.

"He wants me, you dig?! Chester L. Simmons, to find the Golden Stool for him. I almost shat granola crumbs when I heard that. Why me?

"And then the Asantehene spoke, or rather threw his voice from over in a corner, must've been a ventriloquist, had a voice like a bass conga drum.

" 'I have followed your movement around the outer edges of our continent, I know of your spiritual battles, what you have suffered and overcome,' he says to me in letter perfect, high toned English. 'And it is for these reasons and many deeper ones that I ask you to find the soul of my nation.'

"Behind that he didn't say another mumblin' word, he just sat there, just as cool and serene as you please. The linguist held a medium sized leather pouch out to me and I crawled out on my hands and knees, the way I'd crawled in. I mean, like that's the way you came to the Asantehene.

"Once I got outside, about five blocks from the palace, I opened the strings to the pouch and discovered it was filled with gold dust. Gold dust! I was shitless speechless.

"It was like, it was like the Great It had asked you to find his favorite pillow and paid you out front for it.

"Now the thing was, I couldn't say anything to anybody because nobody was supposed to know that the Stool was missin'.

"I mean, like if the Stool was known to be missin', the symbolic heart of the nation, people would start dyin' off, out of sadness or whatever, 10,000 natural catastrophes would occur, in addition to the fact that the Asantehene would be lynched in 46 different ways, along with every member of his family, and his name would be recited forever, as the dude who blew the Stool. You talk about a motherfucker in serious trouble! I ain't talkin' 'bout him, I'm talkin' about me!

"If I succeeded in recoverin' the Stool, no one but the Asantehene and his linguist would know about it. If I didn't recover the Stool, my ass would be in a sling, six feet under and no one would know about that either. I mean, it be a thang, like you don't be failin' when the Asantehene puts you on your job.

"I was so shook up that I went off and drank pink gin for a week, tryin' to find the vision for what I was supposed to be doin'."

He turned the corner of the bottle up and killed it, so into his story that he had forgotten about the other people in the cell.

"Oooopps, sorry 'bout that," he apologized graciously.

"Fuck that, man! Go on, what happened?" Marcus shot in.

"Well, once I got my head together, I started gettin' the kind of logical vibes I needed.

"By the process of elimination, I figured out certain things.

"Number one, no Asanti would be caught dead, or alive with the Stool ... their ... uhhh ... sensibilities just wouldn't know how to deal with it. It would be like havin' God's Ghost locked up in a closet.

"I was pretty certain that none of the other tribal groups had copped the Stool because if they had ... well, if they had, they would've had a war on their hands that would've been guaranteed annihilation for everybody, forever. And ever.

"Havin' gone up 'n down, and in 'n out in my head, who could I settle on that would be insensitive enough, disrespectful enough, vicious enough and cold blooded enough to rip off the soul of a nation?"

"The white boy!" Brian called out.

The Great Lawd Buddha leaned over unsteadily, the potato drippings singing in his skull, to slap Brian's palm with a suave stroke.

"Right! A foreigner! now I really had a problem, the English, currently in power at the time, didn't dig me being in the country in the first place and if I made any too wrong moves, my ass was gon' be in another sling, so I had to proceed quietly."

The sound of a fellow inmate's sudden screaming on the tier below them sliced through Buddha's monologue.

They all tensed up. They knew the sound well.

Someone receiving a "Dear John" letter, or suddenly being overcome by the pressure of the cage surrounding him, or from a thousand other prisoned feelings, had gone insane.

The man, his lungs suddenly lined with steel, screamed until the keepers made their immediate appearance, billy clubs and gas guns at the ready, prepared to beat, gas and drag him off to the Hole, for "rehabilitation."

Buddha accepted another cigarette, his hands shaking slightly. It was important to go on, to fight the bad vibes.

"As we all know," he continued, "money talks, all kinds o' money. So, that's what I put to work for me. That, and my game.

"It took me something like two months to find out how many, which and where foreign archeological expeditions had been, or was diggin'. I had cornered things down to that. Since no one had ever seen the Stool, other than the Asantehene, I figured that some fool archeologists, rapin' the country like they was doin' in those days, had stumbled across the piece and was definitely keepin' it cool 'til they got it out of the country.

"Using the elimination process again, I sifted the expeditions ... a French group, an Italian group, a Portuguese group, of all things, and about eight English groups, naturally.

"Gentlemen, you talkin' 'bout a dude earnin' his dust! I sho' 'nuff earned mine that year. I wheeled and dealt my way to the Stool, all boxed and on its way to Rome, two days before the S.S. Aida sailed.

"What I did was this: I found out that the Italians had stumbled across the Stool, which was buried, had lied to the English colonial-master-guys about what they had found and was gettin' ready to arreviderchi.

"Awright, playin' the game, I managed to slip word in to the Head Englishman in Charge.

"Naturally he's severely pissed off.

"I mean, like they were gonna put all the dagos in jail 'n shit ... but what he was really super happy about was get-tin' his grubby hands on the Stool!

"As y'all know, the goddamned English had fought a war with the Ashanti over the Stool, years back, so they really felt groovy about gettin' their hands on something that they'd fought like dogs for. But heyyy, this *is* the Great Lawd Buddha, right?!"

"Right on, Buddha! Right on!" Brian yelled, oblivious to his surroundings.

"Yessuh, so what I did, with about eight of the most nerviest Ashanti dudes you ever thought about hearin' about, was perform the most perfectly executed rip off in the history of the country.

"One of the dudes who helped me rip the Stool off later became a top dog in the government, after Ghana became independent.

"The dudes who was in on it, incidentally, refused to be

paid.

"My con to them was, you dig? I want you all to help me pull off a fantastic, unreal, daylight holdup on the English.

"That's all I had to say to those dudes, that's all . . . that we were goin' to embarrass the English so bad that they would be walkin' 'round with red faces, for days.

"And that's what we did. I organized a tribal festival that involved the Asantehene, with his connivance, of course. And while he's layin' his blessin' on the building the festival revolved around, with the Duke 'n Duchess, the King's representatives in attendance who just happened to be in town.

"This is what we did. At the high point of things, my hip Ashanti buddies eased off with the Stool on their shoulders, in a crate, singin' 'n drummin' 'n shit, in the middle of about fifty 'leven million fellow tribesmen.

"I'll never know for certain, but I think . . . I say, I think, the English knew what was goin' down but they couldn't scream, 'Hey! Bring that bloody Stool back!' on account they couldn't admit they had it, not with all those brothers out there.

"On the other hand, the Asantehene couldn't admit that he was stealin' it back 'cause he was never supposed to have lost it in the first place.

"We wound up with what you might call an impasse.

"Three days after the grand theft, the Asantehene called me in again, laid another bag o' dust on me without sayin' nary a word. Two days after that the English advised me to get on.

"Or, as I remember the way the young blonde stud put it, 'Uhhh, Simmons, we should like to see you depart on the next shedlued ship from the ahrea'."

"When's that?" I asked.

" 'This afternoon,' he told me and didn't blink once.

"So, once again . . . there I was, orphaned in the world."

He stood and stretched, "Yeahhh, orphaned in the world."

He bowed to the men in the cell as though he were a Mandarin lord and strolled onto the tier passageway, heading for his own cell, and the horrors awakened within himself, from a couple hours of story telling.

"Buddha!?" Marcus called to him as he made his suave exit.

He turned, a cell away, a quizzical expression on his Benin-Mao shaped face.

"Buddha, you ever think about doin' your autobiography?"

Buddha gave him a cold smile.

"Yeah, I did once, it got all messed up, that's why I'm in here."

Marcus looked down at the floor helplessly, and back up to see Buddha disappear into his own cell, ready for the evening lock up.

He buttoned the top button of his rough, heavy woolen pajamas, pulled his blankets up under his chin and laced his hands behind his head, gazed through the barred cell window at the bristling stars beyond.

He shivered slightly, not from actual cold, but from the thought of it.

Never could stand the cold too well, always loved the warm more.

He looked away from the squared off picture of the bright moon and stars, over to his writing table, a small wooden version of a card table, ignoring the loud, snuffly noises of his cellmate, Ranklin C. Jones, hold-up man, dreaming on his bunk against the opposite wall.

Buddha lay wide awake, filtering the hundreds of midnight jail house sounds through his consciousness . . . the snoring, whispered escape plans, blues hummers, coughers, the squealings of homosexual assaults, the groans and grunts of homosexual relations, the dazzling array of mad sounds that could only come from caged men.

29

He sat up on the side of his bunk, feeling restless, feeling the urge to write.

He smiled at the thought as he pulled the table across the narrow distance to his knees, draped his blankets over his shoulders and sat, alternately staring through the window and down at the notebook and pencils on the table in front of him.

He finally opened the notebook, frowned at the smudge marks on the first five pages, a legacy of Ranklin C. Jones' surreptitious interest, and read up to where he had stopped writing the night before.

"I think the geography book is what carried me off into fantasia, in the beginning."

He picked up one of the pencils beside the notebook, checked the point in the bright glare of the moonshine, no need for the lamp, and began to write, the moon and stars seeming to offer more light with the formation of each word.

"How could I *not* be carried off, in the Beginning, down there in that racial swamp?"

He stirred his pencil around in mid air for a few seconds, mentally reviewing the six lynchings he had watched from a distance during his boyhood, and the far more numerous ones he had managed to escape from, acting "uppidy" in Miss'ssippi, Amerikkka.

"Yes, it was the geography book that carried me off," he continued, "reading about far away places and other kinds of people. Anything would have done it," he thought as he wrote, "anything at all, a soft word, a gentle look, electric lights, an indoor toilet, maybe the hooting of a midnight flyer, but it was none of these, it was the geography book."

Settling into stride, he crossed his ankles and pulled the blankets tighter around his shoulders.

"God only knows how I came across the damned thing, if my memory serves me correctly, we only had twelve books in our whole big one room schoolhouse and none of them had a range of thought beyond Lil' Black Sambo, the Family in the Cotton Fields and such like, but one day, as such things do happen . . . there it is . . . tattered, battered and readable, with pictures yet.

"I can recall even now, oh so clearly, how pissed I was to come to the African section of the book and find all the people looking so black and strange. But that was many years ago, thank God! And I've since developed a more sophisticated view of blackness."

He paused, smiling, as he watched Ranklin C. Jones moan and sensually rub his testicles.

"Everything was strange in that book, the people, the words (it took me quite a while to understand some of them, geopolitics, for example) the names, all of it! That is, until I began to make my own framework for all of it.

"I find myself constantly referring to something I call the Beginning.

"For want of a better word, I guess I'll have to stay there, for a few emotional beats, before I go on to the upper levels of purgatory.

"The strong, always tired, black, dirt working robots who happened to be my parents and all of the relatives who looked and acted pretty much as they did, were not the Beginning, nor was that clapboard shack with the old newspapers wadded into the cracks, nor was the white man who had the power of life and death over us.

"No, it was the aroma of places I'd never smelled, the look in a pair of eyes I'd never seen, the urge to wander around inside my soul . . . that was the Beginning.

"Once released from my extended bondage by the power of the book, I wandered around the world, doing the undoable; I slept with the white women, blondes, in defiance of all of Miss'ssippi's rules.

"I climbed Fujiyama, looked the sacred leopard on the top

of Kilimanjaro in the eye, ran with the bulls of Pamplona, went off into fern coated shacks with Polynesian goddesses who nursed me through tropical fevers, killed lions and elephants for the favor of the hand of the Oba's youngest daughter.

"I emigrated to old China on a dilapidated freighter and found myself on the southside of Chicago, in the middle of the winter time.

"But what did it matter? After I found that the only thing I had to do was open up a dozen, a hundred, a thousand other books that would sweep me away just as quickly."

A heavy bank of clouds oozed across the moon's face, temporarily darkening his effort.

He waited impatiently for it to pass, aware, once again, of the richness of night noises in the pen.

Somebody typing on the tier below . . . must be Kwendi.

Yeah, that would be him, young stud never sleeps it seems, with all that revolutionary stuff on his mind, but who am I to talk about people not sleeping?

The clouds passed, leaving him blinded by the re-emergence of the moonlight.

"Leaving Miss'ssippi three steps ahead of the lynch mob and working, bumming, conning, doing whatever else necessary to make life happen was a great book.

"I wish I had the nerve to try and remember all of it. Starving almost to death in a hermit's shack down in Cairo, Illinois. Why Cairo, Illinois? My imagination said to me. Why not Cairo, Egypt? And I was off . . . the one room shack became a fifty room hashish den owned by a funky but Ptolemic aristocrat.

"It's a very strange thing to admit to yourself, after so long, that you are a liar.

"But I wonder about me, specifically me, on this score. Have I really been a liar all these years, or a geography teacher?"

He frowned at the sound of the toilet being flushed in the next cell.

"What does it really matter? After all is said and done, about what you are, someone once said, it's what you have done with what you are. And what was I before I was tamed? Had the iron doors slammed behind me and the key thrown away?"

The moon glared at the fierce smile he turned up to it.

"What was I? A question that not many men as wise as myself would even attempt to deal with."

He paused, on the verge of writing a lie, before going on with the truth.

"I was a conning, cunning, scheming, dreaming, shrewd, slick, conniving beast, a miniature dinosaur with a huge brain ... a lecher, a consummate player ... I was, at one time, the hippest of the hip."

He had to stop writing for a moment, to cool out the gush of egotism he felt rising within himself.

"Yes, at one time, I was me, a supersonic, geopolitical mac-man. There've been times when I've found myself flashing across the face of the planet, taking those who could come with me, on the strength of a name ... Yemen, Jakarta, Hunza, Moeshoeshoe, Lhasa, Huatabampo, Mundina ... God! Whatever happened to Mundina? Yes, if not the name of a place, the name of a woman, or her perfume, or the shape of her earlobe.

"I was that, a lover of the lives of the women who thought that the greatest gift they had to offer was their bodies and all I really wanted, in most cases, was their stories."

The sour-sweet memory of "Heatwave" set off a dull, achy feeling around the region of his heart.

"The ladies of my summer in life, the Circassians, the Navajos, the hundreds of hours of glamorous sorrow I suffered, taking my grizzled lovebone into and out of their holy slits, putting my mind into the position of being given something more precious than all the cunt they could possibly lay on me.

"Back and forth I've gone, across these United States, from east to west, from north to south, tripping into Mexican villages, near Detroit, or raiding the striped tents of rival Bedouins because that's what the book said one should do, just this side of the Golden Gate Bridge.

"The moments I've had, the exquisite flavors of ten thousand make do stews in a thousand hobo jungles, the glistening stories recited by shattered men with hearts of tempered steel, the little campfires, the rivers of cheap wine."

He let the pencil slip out of his fingers and leaned back against the wall, wishing he had a cigarette.

He peered across at Ranklin C. Jones, at the silly smile slicing his brown face in dreamland, probably dreaming of Pam Grier's titties, checked out the area surrounding him and spotted a half smoked cigar in a jar lid under the edge of his bunk.

O well, what the hell . . .

He skirted the edge of his table, stooped for the half done stogie, found a match and lit up, frowning from the first puff. Guess beggars can't be choosy.

He remounted his seat behind the table, the smoke from the cheap cigar, held down too long, giving him a cheap high.

He looked closely at the last words he had written, "rivers of wine, rivers of wine, days and nights of frustration, illness, suffering, a lifetime of dismal failure. How hard it is to tell the truth. A lifetime of failure. To be able, after all these years, to say that. To say that I've never been to Europe, Africa, Asia, or any other fuckin' place outside my country 'tis of thee."

He dropped the smoldering cigar butt on the floor, feeling

angry with himself.

"Made it up as I went along, that's what I did. I made it all up, the windblown feasts on the Mongolian steppes with kurdish tribesmen ... here's yogurt in your eye!

The Japanese Penis Worshipping Society, Chester L. Simmons, aka the Great Lawd Buddha, President ... down, girls, down! The voudoun thang in Papa Doc's Haiti, Ogun's ride on my head, my career as a nudist photographer on the French Riviera, the kisses I exchanged with the princesses of twelve nations, including that coldblooded young English bitch who loved horses more than she liked men.

The rackets, the games, the schemes, the hustles ... all lies!"

He looked up, surprised to see the sky streaked by the first signs of another day, in this instance, Thursday, but no matter, they were all the same in the joint. He hurried on, writing as though the full day would destroy everything he had written.

"My life has been one glorified lie, from Beginning to End. A lie that deviated from time to time but still remained a lie, or maybe I should put it another way, where other men have habitually told the truth and lied sometimes, I have always lied and told the truth as seldom as possible—"

"What's happenin', Buddhaman?" Ranklin yawned across at him, ending his story for the moment.

Buddha nodded his head neutrally, plastering his opaque look on.

"You been writin all night again?"

"That's right, brother, all night long."

Raklin stepped onto the floor gingerly, tip-toed over to the unenclosed stool to relieve his bladder.

"Mannnn, I don't see how you do it, I have a helluva time tryin to scribble my woman a few lines every now 'n then."

Buddha smiled and, with the rest of the stirring inmates,

prepared to deal with another jailhouse day before the breakfast gong.

"Buddha?" the guard called to him through the bars.

"Yeah, what can I do for you, Smitty?" Buddha turned to him casually, folding his blankets on his bunk, looking forward already to the nap he was preparing to steal later in the day.

"Warden wants to see you."

Buddha straightened up, a shrewd gleam spooling the possible reasons why around in his mind.

"What's he want, Smitty?"

"Tell ya the truth, I don't rightly know."

Ranklin winked off side at Buddha, turned to the guard, working sour against Buddha's sweet.

"What the fuck you mean, you don't know! You the motherfuckin' po-lease here, ain't you?"

"Awright now, Rank! You'd best mind your own business, when I got somethin' to say to you, I'll call your name 'n number, okay?"

Ranklin C. Jones, having spent a night dreaming of freedom and fast ladies, started to bristle up at the guard. Buddha, cool, cooled him out.

"Rank, it's cool, baby, warden probably needs my help to figure something out. I'll be ready in a minute, Smitty."

He changed into his pressed prison denims, brushed his teeth and shot a natural comb through his receding hairline a few times.

"Okay, let's be gettin' on."

Smitty signalled to the control tower and manually unlocked Buddha's cell door.

"Better watch your step, Rank," he grumbled through his slipping upper bridge.

"Shhhh-it! If you know what's good for you, you better watch your own fuckin' step. This is our prison, not yours."

Buddha and the guard fell into step, on the way to the warden's office, Buddha mentally reviewing his sins of the past week.

Wonder what the fuck he wants to see me about? That cocaine deal? Nawww, he wouldn't have any way of knowing about that. The prostitution set up? Nawww, it wouldn't be about that, what the hell do they care about punks setting up a union?

The moonshine still in the kitchen. Naw, not that either, that's been there for years. What?

He maintained a poker face through all the check points, began to feel slightly nervous as they stood in front of the huge paneled door of the warden's office.

Smitty knocked politely, twice.

"Come in!" a big bass voice boomed.

"The Great . . . uhh, Chester Simmons, sir," Smitty announced, ushering him in.

"Come in! Come on in, Buddha. Uhh, thank you, Smitherson, that'll be all."

The guard reluctantly departed, certain that this man he guarded everyday, this passive storyteller, was going to harm his warden in some way.

Buddha stood in the center of the floor, holding his cap behind his back, taking the warden's psychological measure. Big, bluff, bleary eyed beer drinker, three months in the Chair, tough as nails.

"Sit down, Buddha! Sit down! I know you're wonderin' why I wanted to see you. Coffee?"

"Yes, thank you, sir."

The warden bounced over to his intercom.

"Pasquale, two espressos, please."

The Great Lawd Buddha relaxed, placed his cap on his left knee . . . espresso, shit! Things couldn't be too bad, not if he was going to be treated to I-talian coffee beforehand.

The telephone buzzed twice before the warden snatched it up. Trouble with a couple members of the population.

"Sock both of the bastards in the hole!" The warden growled, looking at Buddha as though he were a fellow warden, someone who understood the problems of managing the Big House.

Pasquale, the warden's personal servant, knocked lightly and popped in balancing a tray of coffee cups and a pot of coffee like the good Italo-European waiter he had been, once upon a time.

"Pasquale, I don't wanna be disturbed for the next half hour." The warden warned him as he pulled his swiveling armchair around to the front of his desk to sip with Buddha.

He handed him a demitasse, his ham hold folding over the tiny receptacle, poured one for himself and settled his beefy frame into his seat opposite Chester L. Simmons.

"Now then," he growled jovially, "lemme hear this story about you ruling the city of Tel Aviv for a week without anybody knowing about it. Anybody who can put anything over on them goddamn Jew bastards has got to have a helluva lot on the ball! Hahhh hahhh hahhh hahhh ... "

The Great Lawd Buddha settled back in his seat, extremely distressed about the role he was being forced into, balanced his coffee cup on his thigh, an enigmatic smile on his face.

Uhhh huh, so this is what this mad motherfucker wants, a Scherharazade session, huh? Oh well, espresso is a helluva lot tastier than that chicory dishwater in the mess hall. Guess I better tear that shit up I wrote last night, no one would believe it anyway.

He suavely held his cup out for a refill, pinky finger extended.

"Well, warden, you see, it was like this. I had copped a ride on this ol' broken down freighter, deliverin' coffee from Brazil to Haifa and ..."

Chapter 2

The Telephone Freak

He slumped back into the glum comfort of his favorite chair, nursing an afterwork can of Coors, studiously checking out the articles in his one bedroom efficiency apartment.

The drab, last-century woodland scenes framed by dark strips of paneling, the worn, semi-Persian rug, the full moon paint job flaking from the ceiling in all four corners. Two windows faced a smoggy Los Angeles evening and a street lined with strangers.

Finally, unable to avoid it, his attention glued itself to the telephone on the table at his right elbow, and the sheet of notebook paper under it. He plunked the can of beer down beside the phone, jolting a bit of the brew from the can, and snatched the paper from underneath the telephone paperweight.

With the paper in his hand, he leaned his head back against the top of the chair and moaned . . . a soft, drawn-out, primitive sound.

Who would be likely to be at home? 6:00 p.m. Housewives cooking dinner. "Career" women. People home from work. Whoever.

He dug his hand down into his crotch, pushing and stroking his developing erection. Always developing . . . always trying to develop.

He raised the paper to chest level and squinted at it.

Seven names and seven phone numbers, picked at random from the phone book, using the flip-the-page open and stab method.

His hand shook slightly as he reached for the beer can, a sip before dialing the first number on the new list.

The voice that answered was weak and uncontrolled, disconcerting. He took a couple deep breaths into the receiver and hung up, his brow beaded with instant perspiration.

"Who was it, Tommy?"

"Somebody breathin hard, Mom," Tommy answered, waddling along on his five year old legs, not giving a second thought to the caller.

Mrs. Manson smiled, as usual, at her precocious son, turned over a couple potato-yam pancakes and wondered how long it would be before the man of the house arrived, with a pocketful of panhandled monies and a few good stories about the actions and reactions of square people.

Living on a flute-played-in-the-street budget was not always lucrative, but inevitably interesting.

He held his hand on top of the phone, momentarily disgusted, but at the same time intrigued by the voice that he had dialed out of nowhere. A damned baby's voice. He felt his quivering erection melt away.

40

A few minutes of heavy thought pushed him back up to par, he dialed the next number on the list, hung up before anyone answered and scurried over to his tape recording setup.

Music for a background, that always supplied a little something extra. He fumbled nervously removing the tape from the machine . . . a full hour of recorded "Hello? hello? hellos?" "Who is this?" "Hello?" "Speak!" and other assorted responses to his past calls.

His favorite cuts were the ones that had women gasping, or sounding instantly hysterical as they listened to his obscene proposals.

Calmer now, thinking of his experiences, he threaded a new roll of tape onto the machine, placed The Julliard String Quartet rendition of the Ravel *Quartet in F Major* on his portable and started both machines. The tape ready to receive, the portable spilling out the lush, plunked notes of Ravel.

He carefully placed the microphone on the table and slowly eased back into his chair.

A smile flitted across his face. Beautiful.

He liked nothing better than to stage a call, alternating effects from time to time.

Epstein, Charlotte, Jewish. The name simply indicated a religious preference. He cared less about the religious thing. If a little fantasy did exist in this case, it had to do with the possibility that she might have big breasts. Like, Lainie Kazan, maybe.

"Hello?" the voice said calmly, once, twice, three times, and then the edge of panic crept in. He placed the receiver beside the microphone, mentally adding the elements that were being fed onto the spool of tape. *The Quartet*, a woman's voice saying "Hello?" and the harsh sound of a man huffing into the phone like a panting dog. He hung up, not bothering to check if she were still on the line.

He slumped back into the chair, feeling frustrated, confused. There were no guarantees in this business, each call was apt to have either a roller coaster feeling or a dull thud.

He strolled over to stop the tape, rewind and play it back. "Hello? ... hello? ... hello ... hel-low? So what is this, some kinda game, with music yet?" click!

Beautiful voice. Paid no attention to the animal sound, or she overlooked that to hear the music. New York Jewish-accent-dialect ... ha.

He strolled through the apartment to his small kitchen-alcove for a fresh beer, his face flushed with the warm feeling of what he liked doing more than anyting else in the world ... freaking off on the telephone. He popped the opener on the can. No comparison to anything, not even sex. Shit! It *was* sex!

He took a long sip, started the tape, changed the music to fit the next call. A Spanish name ... something Latin ... for a Spanish name.

Mrs. Epstein sat in her cozy little apartment at the Shalom Retreat ("A Little of Israel in America"), her firm Ashkena-zic brow wrinkled with deep thoughts.

It couldn't possibly be him? Or could it? Her thoughts were rippled at different points by Yiddish question marks. Would he be likely to approach her in such a way? One could never tell. The older men nowadays, even, took a lot of pride in different approaches.

She stood in front of her bedroom mirror, feeling the slightly wrinkled surface of sixty five years of life. Not bad ... not bad.

Impulsively she decided to do something else with her hair.

The Shalom Retreat had an inner-inner reputation for a cer-tain kind of chic, best displayed at the four card tables that shuffled into action at 6:15, sharp.

Rearranging her hair once again, subconsciously into the

style that it was originally, she sprayed a light, flirtative base of perfume behind each ear, and, in a sudden display of devil-may-careness, behind each knee.

Alright, Mr. Seymour Weintraub, latest greybeard Heart-throb of the Retreat, if you want to play games on the telephone, I'm your match. Off to the retreat rec room.

"I wanna fuck you and suck you and stick my dick into your asshole, you little sweet honey pussy bitch!"

He hung up, the muscles twitching in his throat, sweat coursing down both sides of his face in twin streams. He had not meant to say what he had said. It just simply pulled itself out of him, in nervous, jerky spasms. A girl's voice, light Spanish accent, Chicana, sexy. The sudden vision of a brown body with long, wavy black hair falling onto lush, melon-shaped buttocks had done it.

He played it all back, his hand trembling around the beer can, the front of his pants spotted from an emission. Always emissions, never ejaculations.

It didn't shoot out, it oozed out.

An almost feathery voice, unexperienced, a virgin voice. He replayed the section again, the spot growing larger.

God! What a voice!

He replayed the "Chicana" section, as he mentally labeled it, twice more. There was never any way of knowing which ones would bring it out, not even after two years.

Two years of, what did *they* call them? Filthy telephone calls. He slid away from the media's description of his kick. What the hell do any of them know about feelings, about being onto a supersonic method of communication? Bunch of ordinary bastards who haven't gotten beyond the missionary position. If we could all get our thrills like this, there wouldn't be any rapes. Or a bunch of other perverted crimes. What the hell is bad about a phone call?

43

He drained the can and went for another one, and a ham sandwich, feeling vaguely satisfied, but unable to stop his compulsion from running its course.

"Ayyy! . . . Aaayyyy!"

"Whassamatter, Dolores?" seven year old Juan Martinez asked his teenage sister/babysitter.

He was joined by the next in chronological line, his five year old sister, Estrella.

"Yeahhh, whassamatter, Dolores . . . why you holdin your head like that?"

Dolores Martinez, fifteen year old Catholic Mexican-American virgin, slowly uncupped her ears to hear the questions being asked.

What could she explain to her little brother and sister? They wouldn't understand. She felt like screaming.

"Why you act so fonny, huh?" Estrella probed, jerking on her arm.

"She's got a boyfriend," Juan slipped in slyly, playing the devil's advocate.

"Yeahhh, she's got a boyfriend," he said again, more positive this time.

"Dolores got a boyfriend! Dolores got a boyfriend!" they chanted at her, circling around, making a game of something they didn't relate to. Coming back to herself, she made a vain attempt to get into the spirit of their innocent fun.

"I'll boyfriend you!" she screamed in the jocular tone of voice that seemed to elicit instant, delighted yells from them every time, as she chased them through the house and into the back yard.

She paused at the back door, wondering, why? Why me? Lots of people get these kind of calls, but why me? I'll have to go to Mass and Confession more often, she thought, hopping down into the yard to play with her brother and sister.

44

Dirty, filthy gringo! No decent Mexican dude would ever think of doing something like that.

She froze in place after two steps, the sudden, chilling sound of the telephone ringing in her ears again.

"What? You wanna do what? Fuck? When? Where?"

He slammed the phone down and stutterstepped over to the tape recorder to snap it off, knocking his beer can over in his haste.

Filthy bitch! Who in the hell did she think she was?

His state of mind, swimming in a brewer's haze, went from quick anger to burning indignation.

Pig!

He rewound the tape, played it back.

"Listen to this, bitch! I want to fuck you and . . . "

"What? You wanna do what? Fuck? When?! Where?"
Click!

He stood staring down at the tape, chewing on his bottom lip.

He felt an ugly, nauseous feeling swell in the pit of his stomach. The woman's voice was so much like his mother's that he had to stifle the urge to puke.

That same hard, raspy tone . . . the super quick response.

He quietly took notice of the spilled beer, cleaned it up with a bathroom sponge, the telephoning forgotten for the moment.

He settled back in his chair with a fresh can.

Yeahhh . . . like Mom's voice.

"Alexander, goddamn you! I'm going to tell your father when he gets home and we'll see what he has to say about you disobeying me!"

Yeahhh . . . like Mom's voice.

A trickle of beer ran down the side of his jaw as he smiled while trying to take another sip, the irony of how his last call

45

had backfired on him acting as the catalyst for his amusement.

I'll have to call her again. The pig! I'll bet she weighs three hundred pounds and has a snout.

Ms. Marsha Cooke, lotus positioned on the floor in a shortie nightgown, already bent out of shape, poured another half water glass of King's Ransom and laughed bitterly, her eyes straying from the fantasy of the 6:30, early bird movie.

Her fingers, frozen into splayed positions by six straight water glasses of scotch, shook slightly as she lit a cigarette.

Who could it have been? Brian? Marvin? Quincy? Parnell? Richard? One of the others?

Tears mingled with the taste of the whiskey. What the hell did it matter? Some fucker wanted to fuck.

Drunk, she accidentally mistook his whiskey glass for an ashtray, laughed aloud at her mistake and drank from it anyway.

A fucking telephone freak. I guess I don't deserve any better.

She hunched herself closer to the phone, tears spilling out in a soft stream, wishing that he would call back. Or that someone would call.

Deciding suddenly, midway through his fifth can, to call a man, he scratched out the name of the next woman on the list and reached for the telephone book.

A ... B ... C ... D ... D for dick. *Daddy, don't ...*

He clumsily underlined Daniel Dawson. What could be better? Not one D, two Ds.

He copied the number from the book onto his paper, slugged the rest of the can down and dialed, stage effects temporarily forgotten.

A deep, bullish voice answered. "Yeah?"

The sound floating out of his throat seemed to come from

46

another being.

An animal, a hyena, or maybe a wounded coyote.

And then the words: "Remember me, Daddy? Remember me?"

He gently replaced the receiver, hating himself for not having the tape on.

That must've really freaked the big ol' strong, deep-voiced bastard out!

He tried to make the sound again, to practice it, but it wouldn't come . . . only softly muffled screams, someone choking on himself.

Have to try it again. With the tape on this time. One more beer left.

He flipped the pages, his associative forces operating so subtly that he didn't realize that he had picked the name Hobbs because something was bothering him deep in the gut.

He lurched through his apartment, feeling sober, for the last member of the six pack, the watery intoxication of the beer allowing him to forget that he was balding at thirty, developing a punch from nightly beer busts, and that he was desperately lonely.

Returning from the kitchen, he bumped into the bathroom door on his way in. He stood holding the limp muscle with one hand, tilting the can with the other hand.

Calculating that he was ridding himself of at least three cans of beer, he decided to skip the middle part by pouring a few dollops over the head of his penis.

Not the same thing, he thought, not the same thing at all . . . miss all the fun that way.

He shook as many of the excess droplets from himself as he could and then stuffed it back into his pants hatefully, as though he were trying to push the ugly face of a snake away.

The front of his pants damp from residual urine and crusted from flawed semen, he returned to the other room.

47

Mechanically, with the overly precise movements of an expert drunk, he thumbed through his record stack, looking for something . . . something blue and jazzy.

Miles Davis . . . an old cut, *Kind of Blue*. What could be better?

Creating an elaborate production out of placing *Kind of Blue* underneath the Latin album, topped by the *Quartet*, he found himself praying silently. God . . . let it happen. It happened a couple times and I was alright for a long time. Let it happen again . . . please . . .

He pushed the reject switch on the portable and switched the tape to record. Mistakenly, his mind occupied with the lovely talk he wanted to make into some woman's receptive ear, he copied the number for Clarence Hobbs instead of Christine.

Making a last check of his equipment, he took the phone from the table and stretched out on the floor.

Nice prologue, he thought, to have this much music on the tape . . . before. He allowed each dial a complete, slow second. Two rings.

"Uhhn huh?" A black woman, Pearl Bailey contralto, sounds like she has something in her mouth. A black woman named Christine, probably having dinner.

Won't she be zapped out by this?

Has to be beautiful with a name like Christine.

"Listen to me close, baby," he began softly, riding each syllable mellifluously, "I know you're going to think this is kind of strange . . . hah hah. Hah hah hah . . . but I have to tell you this, I can't hold it in any longer . . . I love you."

"Who in the fuck is this?" the woman's murmured contralto, suddenly flip-flopping, switched to a dark, male tenor, roared into the telephone. He slammed the receiver down, angry with himself for being caught, for not being able to guess the speaker's sex.

But what the hell could you make out of "Uhhn huh," if it were sort of mumbled into the phone? Nigger! There was nothing he hated more than being caught.

And it happened, unavoidably, sometimes. Like, the damned answering services.

That was like talking, like having sex in a telephone with a prophylactic on the other end.

He slurped the rest of the beer down and sprawled out to listen to the music, the reflected glare of the record label on the ceiling making him think of Raquel Welch.

"Yo' nigger just called! or whatever he is. Ain't no tellin 'bout you, you might be givin it up to anybody!"

"Clarence, what on earth are you talkin about?"

"Don't try t' nut out on me, you know damned well what I'm talkin 'bout ... the son of a bitch that I just got through talkin to that thought *I* was *you!* that what I'm talkin 'bout!"

Geraldine Hobbs shook her head and rolled her eyes to Heaven with exasperation. Lawwwd! this man!

First, he lies and tells me that he's scheduled for the evening shift, leaves for work at 6:30 in the morning, gets home at 4:30, and now he's going to try to con me into believing that my boyfriend just got through rappin with him. Bob wouldn't dare call here!

Why in the hell did I ever marry such a jealous ass ...

"Well?" Clarence took his most aggressive stance, John Henry muscled arms folded across his Jim Brown shaped chest.

"Well, what?" she answered-asked, looking up from her five-five to his six-one.

She watched the muscles coil up in his throat and wished, for the flash of a moment, that he would reach down and slap her. But he wouldn't. She knew that.

He would rant and rave and afterwards, they would make

love, ferocious love. Jealous ass . . .

"Clarence, I don't have the slightest idea of what you're talkin about! Now look! I just went through all the trouble of fixin you exactly what you asked me to fix you for dinner, and you gonna stand around here lettin it get cold, talkin about some . . . some mysterious lover o' mine."

She made a smartly executed wave away from him to the kitchen, knowing that he would automatically trail her to a dinner of barbequed ribs, spaghetti, cole slaw and corn bread, peach cobbler optional, cold lemonade or beer on the side.

He stomped behind her, his demand to know who her lover was growing less insistent as they got nearer the kitchen.

Who in the hell did he talk to? she wondered absently.

He scuffled up from the floor, shuffled over to the tape and snapped it off, the tail end of the spool slapping to a stop.

9:30 p.m.

He stood, swaying and yawning in the center of the floor, a vaugely disordered feeling surrounding his movements.

Gotta piss.

The hardness caught him off guard, the urine spraying out. He smiled with pleasure and gripped himself with his full hand. The lilt of the Spanish accented voice reeled gently through his mind. Have to talk to her again.

"Clarence, I swear I don't know who that was, or why he called. You know how freaky some people are, they got people who get their jollies like that."

She snuggled up into the crest of his armpit, watching the glow of his cigarette in the dark, feeling the powerful thump of his heart, hating and loving him for his jealousy.

"Clarence," she murmured, sliding her left thigh across both of his thighs.

"What?" he finally answered.

"Did you hear what I said?"

"Uh huh, I heard you."

"Well?"

"Well what?"

"Don't you believe me?"

He smashed the cigarette out in an ashtray beside the bed.

Believe you? How in the hell could I believe anything a bitch out of a topless massage parlor said?

"Yeahhh, baby . . . I believe you. I believe you," he answered in a small, faraway voice.

And methodically folded himself on top of her for a solid job of lovemaking. She, responding dutifully with the practiced grunts and moans that he hated, gave as good as she got.

They laid side by side, afterwards, each pretending to be asleep.

Son of a bitch . . . he jumps on top of me like a horse, drops a load and falls over to the side like he done done somethin'. What does he think I am . . . some kind of spitoon?

Whore . . . He clenched his eyes shut and gritted his teeth together on the thought. Whore. Topless massage parlor . . . slut . . . Rudy was right. "You gon' hate yourself *and* that broad one o' these days, Clarence . . . mark my words."

"She ain't no broad, Rudy. And by this time next month she'll be my wife."

"You gon' marry the bro . . . ?"

"You heard me."

"Awwww c'mon, mannnnn, you got to be jivin, you too old to be goin' on this kinda trip."

"What's old about forty two?"

"Well, for one thing, it's seventeen years older than her twenty five."

Lightly, effervescently, two years ago.

"It ain't the first time a big number was put into a smaller one . . . hahhahhah."

51

"I hear ya, brotherman. Well, good luck anyway."

Clarence flashed a mean smile in the darkened room.

"Good luck," a bet on a race horse, a couple words to a boxer, or a track man, or a gambler.

"Good luck." Shit!

Old, dull, conservative, jealous ass bastard. Can't even take a drive to the supermarket without him suspecting me of something. Bet he would shit a brick if he knew about Bobby . . . to say the least. "They calls me Bobby the Spoon and I can make you feel like you on the moon."

So jiiivvve. But at least he's fun to be with, whenever. And he did know how to do more than just jump on and off. Poor Clarence, poor hard-working Clarence. Don't know how to have fun or be lighthearted. So serious, so goddamned jealous.

She flashed back to all the times during the past two years that he had suddenly come home from work, hours ahead of time, or hours after. Alternating shifts gave him the chance to pull off the surprise. but not quite as often as he thought.

All she had to do, the minute he left for work, was call the plant and speak to the time keeper, a hip sister with a jealous dude of her own.

"Nawww, honey, Clarence ain't due in here 'til 4 today."

Inevitably, on those days that he lied and left home at 6:30 a.m., for the 7 a.m. shift, he would return at 10 or 11, to find his hard, house-working wife going about her domestic chores.

But he never gave up. And now, a damned telephone freak.

"Gerry, why did you marry me?"

Truthfully, thoughtlessly, she answered, " 'Cause I wanted to get outa that massage house, with men feelin all over me."

A scream roared deep inside Clarence's gut as he turned his back to her, his eyes glazed with tears that wouldn't spill. My wife . . . the bitch I love.

Dolores Martinez shuffled down the broad steps of the church, her sense of guilt reinforced by confession and a celibate, out-of-tune-with-this-world-type priest, who had severely reprimanded her for bringing the out-pourings of so much sinful conduct down upon herself.

What would fifty Hail Marys do?

Would fifty Hail Marys cancel out the traumas of a month full of telephone freak calls? Would they make her forget the obscenities?

"Have you informed your parents about this matter, my child?"

She stumbled on the next to the last step.

Inform my father? My mother?

Daddy would think I was trying to make up excuses for having made a "bad connection."

Mama? No telling what she would think. What the hell did they teach women in Chapala, Mexico about telephone freaks?

She walked through the streets of her barrio, oblivious to normal happenings. How can I be normal to have such a thing happening to me? Who could it be? Somebody from school? Some crazy dude?

"Eh, Dolores ... what goin on?"

Juan Mendoza, El Marijuanero, they called him behind his back, for his excessive use of the herb. Juan. My little brother's name.

"What do you want, Juan?"

"Nothin, chica ... nothin, can I walk with you?"

"Why not, I'm only goin home."

"Uhh, home? I'll walk you halfway. O.k.?"

She probed, lightly, flirtatiously, "What if I'm not going straight home?"

"Even better, I'll walk you all the way."

Juan? No, it wouldn't be him, he wouldn't do anything like that. "No, don't put your arms around me, Juan ... you're

53

not my novio."

"Why shouldn't I? Who is?"

Shyly, "I ... I don't have ... "

"Then why shouldn't I? Why not me, Dolores? You know I've always liked you ... besides, if we ride ... ?"

She slid into the passenger's seat of his low rider as if she had done it a hundred times before. Why not? If Hail Marys had to be said for somebody making filthy phone calls to her, then why not Juan Mendoza? At least he was real.

She rushed past her parents sitting on the front porch.

"It's nine fifteen, Dolores," her father announced heavily, the all-day cigarette hardly moving beneath his Pancho Villa mustache.

"I know, Papa ... I stopped at church after I left Graciela's house, to light a candle for Grandma."

Mama Martinez' mouth eased into a slight smile at the corners. Dolores was such a good daughter, almost old fashioned.

Dolores stood in front of the bathroom mirror, both hands gripping the face bowl, her knees trembling.

I've sinned ... I've sinned ... I've sinned ... She stripped her jeans and blouse off, feeling more ashamed the more naked she got. The bloody spots in the crotch of her panties flushed tears from her eyes.

They always said it would hurt so ...

"Hey Dolores! hurry up out! I wanna use the bathroom!"

"In a minute, Juanito! In a minute."

She looked around desperately for someplace to hide the ugly evidence of her sin. No place to hide bloody panties in the Martinez bathroom. She hurriedly pulled her clothes back on, feeling as though she were circling her body with something dirty, something obscene, something that everyone could see.

Have to get rid of these tomorrow when they go to work.

54

Her little brother rolled his eyes at her as she strolled out, trying to look nonchalant.

"Papa's right, women take too long in the bathroom, you know?"

She ruffled his hair and smiled, her mind in other places, her heart threatening to thump a hole through her blouse. God ... if Papa found out he would kill me.

"Emma, what's this shit Tommy keeps rappin' about, some dude huffing and puffing on the phone? He been in the stash again?"

"Yeahhh, I smoked some with him earlier today, but that ain't it. Some guy's been calling. He plays music sometimes, but usually he just huffs and puffs. Tommy thinks it's funny."

"Telephone freak, huh?"

"Yeah."

Mark and Emma Manson traded hits on the hash pipe, sprawled out on their bedroom mattress, indulgently taking in the color patterns of the Los Angeles sunset.

"Telephone freaks are really spaced, huh?"

"Yeah. Really."

They went back and forth on the pipe a few more times before putting it aside, simultaneously placing their hands on each other's sex for a soft core session of mutual masturbation ... loaded, unthreatened, feeling groovy.

"Telephone ... freaks ... really ... are ... spaced ... huh?"

"Yeah ... really ... "

"Mrs. Epstein! telephone for you!"

"I'll take it over here, Sarah."

Mrs. Epstein walked quickly across the thick piling of the rec room rug, smiling ever so slightly at Mr. Seymour Weintraub, bridge expert, at table number two, as she headed for the wall booth.

Almost a month of lowered eyelids, shy smiles, gentle "good mornings," "good afternoons" and "evenings" and bolder moves toward real conversations before and after the bridge games.

"You're quite a bridge player, Mrs. Epstein."

"Call me Charlotte, please. You're not so bad yourself, Mr. Weintraub."

"Seymour."

" . . . Seymour."

"Charlotte, I'm tellin you, with my own eyes I've seen . . ."

"Ohh for God's sake, Sophie, behave. You're gushing like a school girl."

"Whatever. But everybody's talking . . . "

"About what they're talking?"

"How he looks at you. Charlotte, he's single, has his own teeth and . . . and he's independently well-to-do."

"Sophie!"

Her best friend in the Shalom Retreat, Sophie Nussbaum, blushed slightly and coughed delicately into a Kleenex.

"Well, it's true. I got the information upon good authority."

Swearing Sophie into complete silence, upon pain of strangulation, Charlotte Epstein whispered, girlishly, into her friend's ear, a calmly dramatized story of Ravel's *Quartet in F Major*, being periodically played for her, on the telephone yet.

"But how do you know it's him?"

"Sophie, if you breathe a word to anybody I'll—"

Sophie Nussbaum shot her eyes skyward and plastered both palms to her full bosom. If I should ever, the gesture said.

"Well, I was in his room the other day . . . "

Sophie clapped her right hand to her mouth and fluttered her left hand back to the heart side, simultaneously.

56

"While he was downstairs, Sophie. While he was down-stairs," Mrs. Epstein patiently explained, "I walked in be-hind the maid, explaining to her that Mr. Weintraub had bor-rowed a record from me and forgotten to return it, if she should be suspicious. And do you know what I found?"

"No, what?"

"Three records from the left, *The Quartet in F Major*, by Ravel."

"So how did you know it was that music?"

"I was married to the second violinist of the Hackensack Symphony Orchestra fifteen years for nothing?"

Mrs. Epstein took careful note of what seemed to be a slightly jealous look in Seymour Weintraub's eyes as she reached the telephone. Bet he thinks I've got a guy on the outside.

"Hello?"

The familiar plunkings and thrommings of the *String Quar-tet* flushed the color from her face. "Oh my God! what . . . ?"

She shot Seymour a quick, frightened look. He returned the look, concern frowning his brow into a question mark. "Hello?" she said again, her knees wobbling a bit. *The Quar-tet* was suddenly interrupted by the receiver being replaced.

He met her halfway across the room. "Charlotte, what's the matter? Are you alright?"

She looked past him with glazed eyes. "Seymour, I have to talk with you about something."

"Come, sit down over here."

Sophie Nussbaum and a few other interested card players leveled surreptitious attention on the tender scene over on the far sofa, the cards momentarily forgotten.

Sophie smiled and sighed. Couldn't happen to two nicer people.

"Whose play is it? Is this a card game or isn't it a card

game?"

"It *is* a card game, Mrs. Nussbaum," the laconic voice of Samuel Fishman, ex-tailor, informed her, "and it's your play."

"No! no! Juan, stop!"

"Awww, c'mon, Dolores . . . you like it, you know you do."

"I'll be gentle, o.k.? I promise."

"Juan? I am your novia now, huh?"

Juan nodded absently, laboring to find a better way to place his feet against the walls of the back seat, mind foggy from three joints of Jaliscan weed.

Afterwards, making certain that their arrangements were squared away for another rendezvous, he dropped her off six blocks from home.

"Take care, baby."

"Good night, Juan," she replied softly and started the slow walk home.

She lowered her eyes passing people on the street. They must see that I'm different now, that I've been making love.

No, not making love, she corrected the thought, fucking. Fucking, like the crazy man on the telephone says it.

Fucking . . .

The hyena laugh and the music and the dirty words that always seemed to catch her. Only her. "Fucking." "Cunt hole." "Bitch." And then whole sentences.

Her legs felt as though they were bumping into each other as she made her way up the flagstones to her house.

"It's ten o'clock, Dolores," her father announced grimly, the cigarette twitching to the corner of his mouth.

"Graciela's mother asked about you today, I saw her in the market," her mother added quickly, "she was wondering why you hadn't been by in such a long time."

Father Martinez removed the cigarette and stared daggers at her. "Tomorrow, we, you . . . me and Mama are making a visit to the doctor."

Dolores looked at her feet, unable to control the flush that changed the color in her face from beige to deep brown.

"Wait a minute, goddamn you! just wait one fuckin minute!"

Impulsively, not saying a word, Stravinsky in the background, he held the telephone a half inch from his ear.

She had caught him, after fifty fleeting attempts. "Are you there? Well, hell yes you are, or else the damned dial tone would ... ohhh never mind! I got a problem too. You're not adding to it or taking away from it, you know what I'm saying?"

What if she's having the call traced? He almost jammed the phone back into its cradle at the thought.

What the hell! it's too damned late now anyway.

This skanky bitch! He listened closely, sipping from his third can of beer. It was obvious that she had been drinking, or was drinking, but it didn't make her slur too much, or sound disordered in any obvious way. If you'd never had had any experience with the kind of person who became more exact, more logical, more ... until they suddenly disintegrated; you'd never know Marsha Cooke's trip. Or Mother's.

"Alex, sit down, let me talk to you for a bit."

"Yes, Mom."

"Alex, I don't know whether you know it or not but I've been having a few problems, quite a few problems over a long period of time. Mostly with voices, strange voices that keep telling me to do different things. I don't know if the voices—"

"Voices?"

"Shut up, goddamnit! while I'm talking. You're so disrespectful, Alex! you can't do anything you're told! How many times have I asked you not to get the knees of your pants dirty? or do this or that, and had you disobey me?"

"The voices ... uhh, what about the voices, Mom?"

"What voices?! What're you talking about?"

"Did you hear me?!"

The sound of the raucous voice in his ear swept him back through the years, back to the present.

"Of course you hear me. Well, what do you say? You carry an umbrella and I'll wear my long red dress, front steps of the downtown library, what do you say?"

"You lousy bitch!" he screamed into the receiver and hung up.

He glared at the telephone, gritting his teeth with rage. Filthy bitch! He flung his half empty can of beer across the room and immediately began to clean up the mess, polishing the telephone with his shirt tail.

Why let a slut like that get to you?

He erased the previous dialogue from the tape. No need to have that creepy bitch's filth on, it doesn't do anything for me. Nothing.

Resettled, with a fresh can, he composed himself for his next call.

See what ol' Dad ... ol' Dan is doing.

Daniel Dawson bit his bottom lip and held his head in his hands. Who? Who could possibly know?

He walked around his apartment checking to make certain that the shades were drawn, drapes in place.

Reassured, he flopped across his bed, the bra strapped across his broad, hairy chest and the tight nylon panties straining across his muscular buttocks.

Who?

The tears started slowly, pulled out of him by a deep sense of frustration and despair. Big Dan Dawson, ex-football player, Sergeant Dawson, twenty year man.

"Don't talkl that shit to me, Sarge ... you're a fuckin lifer."

"Watch your tongue, young man, or I'll have you picking up butts for the next month!"

He turned over on his back, the sudden memory of all the beautiful young bodies he had helped train for war slipping through his mind.

Punk. Fag. Sissy. Queer. Homosexual. Gay.

Could it be one of the guys from the job? Not likely. Most of them took pride in being shortsighted, narrow minded and "masculine." And he was more "masculine" than any of them.

Subconsciously, he flexed his biceps.

No, it wasn't anyone from the job. Who would want to run the risk of jeopardizing his job by calling up the foreman?

He closed his eyes, slipping back through the years, to all the moments and times that he had failed to do what he wanted to do, to be with someone he wanted to be with ...

"Hey Sarge, how many showers do you take a day? Seems like every time I come in here you're here."

"Just trying to stay clean, Lieutenant, just trying to stay clean."

Lieutenant Nelson, short, slim, blond ... beautiful.

What's wrong with being gay?

The thought jarred him to a sitting position.

Yeah, what's wrong with being gay? ... A fag?

He moved slowly from the bed, to shower and shave again.

Why not be what I am? Why not be gay?

Picking through his wardrobe, past the dull blues and browns, for a bright colored shirt and a pair of flame colored pants, he decided to pay the Star Bar another visit.

The first few times had been productive but he had not been able to handle the scene. A mixed bag of pin-striped business types pretending that they had just stumbled in for a martini, semi-hysterical interior decorators trying to show their contempt for women by behaving like semi-hysterical women, full of bitchiness, and the stud crowd, muscles everywhere but under the bottoms of their feet.

Where do I fit? he asked himself, pulling a clean pair of panties on.

Well, definitely not one of the hystericals.

Should I be dominant or passive?

Fluffing his salt and pepper pompadour into place, taking one last look at his smooth, forty three year old cheeks, he decided with a self-revealing nod. Passive. What could be better than that? Than having a strong man tell you what to do, how to do it, and when.

Tripping down the steps of his apartment, he pursed his lips to whistle a little tune, feeling more at ease with himself than he had for a long time.

Both of their heads popped up at the first ring, Clarence's, from a semi-nod in front of the television after a heavy dinner; Geraldine's, from headlines that pointed at the United States as the possible instigator of a Third World War. Anything to beat inflation.

"Answer it," he told her, after the third ring, "Answer it. Don't say nothin but hello and gimme the phone."

She screwed her mouth into a heavy, reluctant frown.

"Goddamnit! you heard me! answer it!" he shouted at her.

"Hello?" she answered on the sixth ring, really worried for the first time.

"What the hell should I do?" she had asked her man-friend, her "husband-in-law," he called himself.

"How in the fuck should I know?"

"But you don't understand. Clarence is damned near out of his mind these days. He really takes these calls seriously. He really does think that I'm tryin to run a game on him."

"Why don't you change your number?"

"Hello?" she said again and then quickly tried to replace

62

the receiver.

Clarence stopped the move with a fierce grip on her wrist.

He took the phone from her hand and slowly raised it to his ear, to listen to an abbreviated version of the *Rubaiyat of Omar Khayyam*, recited in a hardcore porno style.

At the conclusion of the recitation, he calmly replaced the receiver and moved toward his wife.

She started screaming before he reached her, knowing that he had snapped, and that he was going to hurt her, badly.

He skimmed over the column titled, "Man kills wife in jealous rage." From the address given, he could tell that the murder, by strangulation, had occurred in one of the black areas. Niggerville.

He shuddered and gulped a swallow of beer. God! death by strangling. What a helluva way to go.

Quickly going through the daily paper, he decided to have dinner at the neighborhood restaurant, an Italo-Chinese operation, unaware that he had been the catalyst for a crime.

Dolores was blinded by tears and the veil over her face as she solemnly stepped up the aisle of the church, her arm interlocked and trembling on her father's.

For a moment, seeing Juan waiting for her at the altar, shrouded in the light spilling down through the church window, she felt happy. And then it faded, as she came close enough to see the small, frowning lines around his mouth.

"Doesn't she look beautiful?" Someone whispered as she passed.

She stumbled, her mind flicking back to the ugly scenes that were responsible for the moment. The fathers, in one room, over glasses of tequila, lime and salt, deciding that a marriage between their children should happen. And why.

The mothers, in the kitchen, deciding when, where and

what time.

"I don wanna marry her, Papa! I don wanna marry her!"

The words echoed in her skull as the priest intoned the language that would make Dolores Martinez the wife of Juan Mendoza, also known as El Marijuanero. "You gonna be my wife and I don't want no shit outta you," he had told her over the telephone the next day.

She felt as though her clothes were being stripped from her body as Juan pulled her veil back to kiss her, sealing a pact that neither of them was in tune with.

She felt as though she wanted to crawl away, into a deep, dark hole somewhere, as they stood on the steps of the church for pictures of their mutual distress, facaded by icy smiles, pictures that would mirror the mistake they were forced to make, as long as they remained together.

Charlotte Weintraub (she had rifled it back and forth through her consciousness for a week, before feeling comfortable enough to say it slowly) gently settled her holiday-flight-to-Miami-special-rate-glass of cheap champagne onto the fold out table in front of her, and stared into the clouds pensively. Seymour reached over to place his hand over both of hers.

"What's the matter, sweetheart? Worried?"

She nodded her head, no, no, and immediately reversed herself.

"Yes, yes, I am worried, Seymour. What if your mother doesn't like me?"

Seymour Weintraub sighed deeply, and looked even more pensively into the clouds than his newly found wife, and answered: "Momma didn't like me until I moved out, five years ago. You, I'm certain she won't like . . . but that's our cross to bear."

And then he smiled, a quick smile, pathos lurking at both

corners of his mouth.

He broke down midway through her tirade against people who made anonymous telephone calls, refused to leave their names or messages, and promoted strong cases of paranoia in the people they talked to. She was also saying . . .

"Look . . . you have to realize, you wouldn't be a damned telephone freak if the goddamned telephone had never been invented. Now, for the last and final time the public library, downtown? You carry an umbrella and I'll wear my long red dress, the one with the ruffles around the hips, o.k.?"

"Yes, Marsha."

Heyyy baby, the freak called lately?"

"Nawww, either we didn't give him enough to trip on, or he found something else to do."

"Telpehone freaks are really spaced, huh?"

"Yeahhh. Really!"

Chapter 3
Ceta Sisters: A Diary, Sort Of . . .

Legal secretary? Why not? The experience might be useful. I dropped my application in the mail without assuming, for a split second, that I would be one of the chosen.

I mean, after all, I was the individual who was continuously overlooked when it came to grants, funds, scholarships, and all such as that.

I/we had just returned from an eight month devil-may-care-trip to Spain and it was possible to get into a Ceta Program at West Los Angeles City College, and get a salary for attending. (This was, of course, before the U.S. Government became completely hostile.)

Well, what the hell, if you're an African-American writer, you have to believe in Beliefs. A *salary*? Well, after I was accepted ("Lawd H'mercy!") I discovered the joke that "salary" implied.

The real payoff came from my classmates, the forty one women I was going to share the legal secretarial learning experience with. (Yes, the names have been changed, To Protect).

The cloudy face of that peculiar boredom which drives sensible people into acting like idiotic infants sloshed around the classroom once, twice, three times, catching some of us so far off balance that we seemed to be drunk.

Several of us gave into it immediately; Treesha Brown and me for example. A half hour of surreptitious-pseudo philosophical rap-talk-chit chat by the wise old man in the class, telling her something about a lil this and a lil that, the corner of the oldman's urge to suck this lovely young blossom's lips right onto the center of his stinger. Her urge, power-beamed by lustrous, PCP-glazed brown eyes, equally strong.

And what gave the lunch hour to Rougenia's (pronounced Row-gin-knee-ah. Why? Who cares?) abstract flirtation. Real interesting woman, Rougenia; she looks like a cross-section of East Africa, with a heavy touch of Kalahari about the hips. Beautiful sister.

And what suddenly made Lynn and Desiree, the two resident low profile white girls, start throwing paper balls across the room?

As per usual, Oweda and Marie had tripped thru a narcotized lunch hour and were back on the set, sampling nerves, stroking vibes, furnishing Afrikan jibes.

"Grrrrrrl! Wid a ass like yours it must be hard to lay down on your back ... hah hah hah hah hah ... (which is a reeeeel pale imitation of how they laughed)."

Delceen asks me probing questions because she *reeelly* knows what I'm doing, the others have baroque suspicions. She knows ...

"I hope, whenever this thing comes out that you writin

about us, that you'll remember all the bullshit we have to go through."

Typing class. That's the official name of the course, complete with all the typewriters anybody would ever want to steal, but beyond that, behind these machines are the women in the class and here, surreptitiously scribbling frantically about them, this lone male.

They dance in and out of the peripheral picture. I know that Rougenia is sitting in the last seat behind me, on my left, and that we have just shared a dazzlingly complex lunch hour.

She: complexities skipping through every move she makes, smoking a joint and sipping her champale; "Why champale, baby?"

"Cause that's what ladies drink didn't you know that?"

How was I to know that?

Even her girlfriends talk about Rougenia's "abstract" personality.

"Yeahhh, Rougenia? She abstract."

At times she seems almost schizoid; at other times, when she is in real good form, her "uhh huhhhs," "uhhh oohhhs," "naawwwws" and those in between jocularities she makes, are enough to make you believe that she understands Chinese arithmetic. Or think that her mindset was framed on Pluto.

An Afrikan beauty from Deepest Alabama; I can never seem to stop staring at her in the back of my mind because a different facet gleams whenever she turns one way or the other.

The luscious eggplant purple-black lips that rest on a lean, muscular neck that shimmers down into the most spectacularly shaped body this side of Sister Peggy Stevens.

Rougenia knows that she should be somewhere that she isn't, physically, and probably psychologically, but doesn't fully realize how she should get there.

I suspect that that is one of the premises behind the why of why we often say things like, "abstract, like Rougenia be talkin abstract shit."

It is the first day of September, payday, and the day after all the situations. The waters have re-routed themselves, a few of the sisters have started on their periods, the stories have shifted, they reflect different lights, the patterns have been rewoven, the air climbs over a different music.

Wonda makes an Afrik Entrance, swatched in an emerald-paisley Batik-Kente sari. She occupies her space, gesturing gracefully, a full figured dancer in a dream-piece, wrists, lips and two inch fingertips swimming out to instruct the instructor.

The conversation freezes from moment to moment, as the two women measure each other for urns.

That's one interpretation of what they seem to be doing. They could just as likely be talking (psychically) about nuclear physics. Or the cramps that won't surrender to the cramp killers.

My attention shifts . . .

Carmetta slashes and bores through her shorthand book with an evangelistic feverishness that the book, in my opinion, has done nothing to merit. But who am I, a remedial figure, to talk?

Cassandra got to school late today, real late, about two hours. She sits here, her skin glistening like polished chocolate, the silver plated front tooth highlighting the trembling flakes in her black eyes as she sets about the business of making up time.

It's still too early for the spirits to really get let out, but just the right time for things to be happenin.

Desiree suddenly slips (escapes would be a more accurate description) out of the room, on her way to swallow a handful of vitamins.

"Here, take these, they're for everything."

"Damn! How many of these things—?"

"You got twenty six there."

Strange juxtaposition of mixtures, Desiree. She chewed celery stalks for awhile, religiously, a Camel cigarette planted in the left corner of her mouth.

Sometimes she chomps thru a "nastyburger" from the "garbage wagon" alternating health food store raisins and nuts with the cigarette filling up the space between.

Yeahhh, real strange juxtaposition of mixtures, Desiree.

Migraine headaches give her face a drawn, desperate look at times .

"What's wrong, Desiree?"

"I . . . I don't know. I'm seeing clusters of stars on one side of my head and I feel like I want to puke."

A feverish expression seems to be her most natural look, except when she feels playful-girlish, and then something else happens.

Delores (the daughter of a Minister) and I have just exchanged wise-folk looks. She seems to be one of the most innocent people in the world, sometimes.

She has a look about her that was probably cultivated for hours because of her father's position; the mirror-learned look of innocence is rapidly giving way to a wise look, one that she can share with me.

Lynn is wearing black.   Lynn is wearing black. A black crepe rosette perched on the left side of her head, a black network shawl flung across her shoulders, a black bra-halter anded across her pink nipples, a pair of tight black Spanish pants. The effect is dramatic, a coldblooded contrast to her Scotch blondness. (A bit more about Lynn. The girl has Heart. But first off, she's fine. A fine white girl. And this very fact was going to be the reason why her ass was going to get stomped one afternoon.)

Desiree was never confronted with this kind of activity because, well, number one: she was obviously someone "who knew her place" and intended to remain there. Number two: it would be hard to pick on someone who was dropping vitamins, smoking cigarettes, having migraines, and suffering from a severe inferiority complex.

So, the racial thing led to "fine ass Lynn." Several of the sisters corralled her out in the patio and announced that they were going to stomp her ass.

"But why?" she asked, with real innocent look.

"Cause you white and we want to," answered the Neurotic Woman that I always avoided.

"Well, it's impossible for me to change colors . . . " she stacked her books into a neat little heap beside her and fell back into a Sugar Ray Robinson boxing stance.

"Who's first?" she did not ask the question with any degree of resignation. It was definitely challenge time.

The sisters exchanged some real shrewd looks.

The Neurotic Woman tried to egg one of her partners into being first.

"Go head, Sophronia, kick that bitch's ass."

"You do it. You the one who thought this up."

This went back'n forth for a bit til one of the more diplomatic types defused things.

"Awww c'mon, Lynn, you know we was just teasin you, girl. We ain't got no time for all this stuff. We tryin to learn how to type'n shit, so we can get us some good jobs."

That was the end of all that for all time. I'm sure the situation would've been mean for her if she had allowed her ass to be kicked. Respect was granted her stand. Like I said, the girl has heart.

Wonda was just completing one of her marathon monologues. This one was for the instructor, this small, chickenboned white woman with the dark circles under her eyes and the nasalized voice.

She's another white girl with heart, incidentally. We all tried to thump her out of pocket from the first day.

"Miss Watkins, I didn't have time to do my shorthand."

"Not my problem, you've failed your first assignment."

"Miss Watkins, can I be excused?"

"No, and please don't ask again."

By the second week, if the truth is to be shown a fair face, she had won.

"Everybody turn to page thirty two."

Wonda glides to the seat beside me, naturally, imperialistic folds and silk rustling gently, but militantly nevertheless.

A large, fluid woman, perfectly attractive for her size and shape. She must be 5'8 or 9 and about 215. A queen of a woman. She mentions diet in a vague way, every week. I measure her carefully and think it would be a mistake for her to lose more than two pounds.

Her effect on me is Afro-Dreamy-Polynesian. I feel like touching her cheeks from five yards away. Beautifully seductive woman, Wonda is.

We must wander away from Wonda for a couple beats, as I often did, to check out a few of the other sisters in the program.

Sister G.B.: "Together," success oriented, a driven type who knows how to accept shortcomings in others. But can be manipulative as hell if the occasion demands it.

"Did you ... uhh ... did you do your shorthand?"

"Why? Uhh, I just wanted to peek at section two."

Add polished conniver and bullshit artist to the other traits and you have half an idea of who G.B. was/is?

The common suspicion is that she didn't come by her deviousness naturally (that is, streetwise), it was something she had to learn.

Hard working, disciplined, wears her sweaters, jackets, etc., draped on her shoulders. Could it be an indication of her relationship to childhood fantasy number. "Who am I?" Superwoman? Batwoman? The Real Robin? A ten year old wandering home from school?

She is obviously a dedicated woman who would have made a dedicated, profound fanatic if she had decided to play into that bag. Very personable, inspires confidence, knows what she wants.

Strangely, just the other day, I found out that the sister is "saved." It doesn't explain everything but it does give me an insight as to the how/why she is able to take so much bullshit. The religious are often able to do this, I've noticed. I don't always see it as an enviable trait.

From Alabama (yes, I spoke) by way of the streets of Brooklyn. So many layers. I wonder what she thinks of Rougenia? Oh well . . .

C.W. A tactile personality, like someone who is almost blind, yet doesn't acknowledge any of the limitations of that affliction. Something else, this sister.

Despite the fact that she would like to push the sightless issue off into a corner somewhere, it won't disappear. Sorry 'bout that, C.W.

You cannot help but be aware that she is having a bit of a problem with her sight when you see her hold a piece of paper with "normal" print as close to her face as her nose.

Always rushed, always rushing (an administrative personality, but you wouldn't know it from her actions) you get the feeling that she feels behind, wants to catch up. Be ahead, and yet, whether she knows it or not, her lack of sight has placed her in the vanguard of things.

There is nothing patronizing in her urge to do good, no cups of unnatural zeal. She sees stuff to be done that the "sighted" never seem to tumble to; tries to lead but becomes

74

less effective whenever she trips onto that track because the bureaucracy is not ready to go as fast as she wants to follow.

I go on. A real human being. Something of the nun about the sister, someone who has "seen" the fringes of something heavy, and come away from it wanting to aid her fellow creatures.

To be closely observed, this one ...

The half blind, not yet fully relying on the senses that the completely blind would have to depend on, but leaning, nevertheless, into the nuances that blind people have going for them, appreciates the sense of a mood, feeling, or word, to a degree that makes them receptive in a way that few "sighted" people will ever know anything about.

Carmen was her name ...

Her recently hired colleague (did I mention that we're in the counseling section?) is obviously from another bag.

Short, pretty faced, heavily stacked, topped by a Josephine Bonaparte hairstyle. I see a facade, pure'n simple.

Sister probably has, beneath that well designed facade, the qualities that the once eminent sexologist, Ron Dobson, labeled "freakism." I can see all of that and more; I see the Bitch Syndrome.

Maybe it has something to do with the need (that some people have) to prove that they are doing the job. Eichmann stands out as a clear cut example of the Bitch Syndrome.

In the sense that I'm using it, it has no chauvinistic value, it is merely the description of someone who insists on being to the Right of Right, even when there is no necessity for it.

We'll leave it here, no need to carry it into bitchiness, bitchfulness, bitched, bitchy, etc.

Back to Ms. Watkins for a moment, who could've been a bitch but never was. Something real subtle happening here .

I impolitely called her "chickenboned" earlier. Let me amend that to fine boned; yes, fine boned, strong minded and clear headed. Her clear headedness borders on hysteria.

Her hysteria is not pronounced, and is more the result of someone with a logical mind being framed in an illogical picture. It is also suggested that she dropped a valium or two, from time to time. My classmates notice everything.

She made it a point of letting us know that she studies yoga, but what she's about doesn't give her the kind of cool that yoga is reputed to give.

Her relationship with this beer-bellied, sloppy woppy of a guy (he was slipped in behind the back of this beautiful black sister who was actually doing the work, as administrator of the program. One day she was there, as effective as an electric volt, and the next day she was replaced by this white man) is more of a tip off to where she really is, more than any other single factor.

Break Time/10:45 a.m.

Yeahhh, Ms. Watkins, filled to here with mostly drummed up problems ... complications.

The problems/complications (I think) have to do with coming from a certain kind of middle-white-middle class, being programmed to a certain kind of number and finding yourself in a place that doesn't give free play for perfectionistic tendencies.

Clearly, she needs a place in Marina Del Rey for a full expression of her academic wages, a place to deal with people who've already "arrived."

Ms. Turner turns to stare at me for a mad minute. She does that from time to time. Very properly brought up lady, she insisted from the beginning of the term, that we call her, "Ms. Turner."

We had no choice.

La Phenomena has returned, a member of the teaching staff, the hysterectomy performed (I overheard), five pounds down from her fighting weight.

76

(I understand. From time to time, watching her posterior tremble as she writes on the blackboard, I understand.)

The scenery shifts because the ladies move. Some of them wobble, some dance, others prance, some slouch, others pout, others shout, but none of them ever leave you with any doubt that they are Interesting. Row-I-Seat-I-Deanna, the Fashion Plate. She glides in, pretending that she has just stepped out of the pages of Cosmo or Vogue. There is a strong possibility that her personal fantasy places her between those covers.

The sister bristles with intelligence, is extremely persuasive ("give-it-to-me-now!"), is extremely photogenic.

Hard to picture her with the trio of children she says she has. Would definitely like to be a part of the Essence-jet-to-the-Bahamas set .

(She dropped out of the program. I wonder if she ever made it to "Trinidad, baby, Trinidad.")

Carlotta La Blanche, a full blown Earthmother figure who real name might be Lotta Black.

She would make it; "You hear me?" She would make it through walls of fire and fences of steel, "You hear me?" because she is a Determined Individual.

Her devil-may-care front conceals a surrealistically serious side. I expect to see her in an office somewhere, one fine day, exploiting a good situation to the absolute max.

(Full of fire, she dropped out. "You hear me?") Oh, well.

The sister with the Afrikan pigtails fluctuates. She seems to be her own personal stock market; up one day, down the next. Sorta quiet. Reserved would be a better adjective, and opinionated, when she opens up.

It isn't easy to figure out where she's coming from. In a weak moment she confessed, "I'd like to be a writer."

(One day, on a down day, I think, she dropped out of the program. That happened quite often. One day someone would be there and the next day they'd be gone.)

Mary L. Love, no party pooper, this one. Sister is straight out of the most passionate section of N'aw 'Leans, bold, has the most passionate section of Bold, has a flair for the collection of demons that only she can see. The demons push her to overdrink sometimes.

She's afraid of bugs. Strange, she's practically fearless when it comes to dealing with anything human but a ladybug can turn her into a dribblin idiot.

She showed us what rough living can do to a person's hands one afternoon.

"See these hands? I've shoveled lots of stuff with these hands, lots of stuff."

She almost seems to enjoy a tough way of living.

Rozetta. Sometimes Rozetta (she spells it Rosetta, Rositta, Rozitta, Rossitter. I suspect it may not be her real name) gets loaded and becomes a wild, wild world of creatures, behind her extravagantly designed shades, her wonderfully creative hairdos (turbaned/cornrowed/straightened/grilled/fied, etc.) and her real red, red lipstick.

She slurs and lurches a lot when she get loaded. Somebody said she drops red devils, seconals.

This sister has real smelly aura (literally) for a while but thank goodness it's gone now. Real sweet sister, really. Innocent, in an uncalculated way, emotional about life, like she's emotional about shorthand, for example.

She is compassionate, intelligent and would probably make an excellent executive.

Desiree comes back. No, Desiree returns. As a one-eighth Indian (no idea what that means), she looks like an ethnic type that didn't quite make the grade.

Sometimes she looks vaguely Mexican and vaguely a few other things. She never resembles anything Africroid, that much is certain.

That is, unfortunately, her most conspicuous trait,

vagueness.

Today is June 5th, 1978 and I've just noticed that she's pregnant. Just goes to show you how vaguely she carries herself.

Weeks later (we went to school straight thru the hot ass summer, a real crash course) she was no longer pregnant; she either had an abortion or a vague baby. Or maybe she hadn't been pregnant to begin with. See what I mean about vague?

The Black Woman, her name is less important than her look. She could be a Fula Woman, or an upper class Hausa Lady, but down here in the program she is simply a sister with a bad attitude. Real bad.

Haven't seen her in a few days, wonder where she's throwing her tantrums and who she's being nasty to?

Her girlfriend, just as dark, but twice as sweet—tempered forms an interesting contrast. This particular sister laid a weird smoke on me one day, it was liberally laced with PCP and kept me feeling hostile for three days.

"Good mornin, Ovida."

"Good morning?"

Ovida has perfected the art of being able to make just about everything she says sound like a question.

For example: the instructor called the roll and Ovida answers, "I'm here?"

The baby has such beautiful music in her voice. Even today "I'm here?" curls thru my memory like a Sarah Vaughn performance.

She amazed me with her ability to consume astounding amounts of herb and remain lucid. I might ask, how did they smoke so much and drink so much and remain so capable of typing and shorthanding? I was frequently at sea after a lunch hour brew.

They have overcome . . .

Flash! Big Picnic coming up next Friday. Meanwhile there

is today to deal with. 1:15 p.m., the thing that happens after lunch. The rest of the class is trying to master shorthand (and seem to be doing well). I've decide to ignore the whole business. I can't say why. Maybe it's the effect of the two daiquiris I had for lunch. Or maybe just a lazy state of mind gripped me.

That used to happen a lot. I still don't know why.

I sit near Olivia for a few days. Olivia is small, foxy with her moves, quick, loves to dance and pulls signals in like a birddog. Her reponse to almost every happenin is a dance movement. I've seen her dance into the ladies room. Really lovely to watch her twist, turn, sway and undulate. Really lovely.

Mrs. Spiegel, a heavy set Jewish woman who doesn't have to tell you that she's Jewish, has recently joined the class.

The administration has decided that there are some po' white folks in the world too.

The consensus is that Mrs. Spiegel is some kind of spy.

Sonya. Sonya. Sonya ... Sonya is a powdery-banana skinned sister with a truly wonderfully shaped behind.

Rougenia, the Abstract one, told her one day, "Girl you know yo' ass is perfect. You know?"

Everyone has said something like that, at one point or another. I've never been around women who were so objective in their assessments. Ahhhemmm.

Sonya's study partner, Debra, has a keen expression, almost a foxy look. I think it has something to do with her nose. Very courageous sister, very courageous.

She actually stood up in front of the class one day and shouted, "You goddamned people are making too goddamned much noise and I can't study."

The noise still goes on. She dropped out.

The atmosphere is strange, one might say "rarified."

We evolved into a loose grouping of people learning some-

80

thing that some of us didn't know before, in addition to all of the stuff we've learned about each other.

Sometimes the mental processes needed to learn shorthand become absolutely clear to me, other times (most of the time) the quibbles, slash marks and complicated scratchings mean nothing, but I manage to get by pretty well by using my own abbreviated form of writing ... Old Hawk's shorthand system.

My head just flickered beyond Gregg, back to a sun blanched cafe in Spain. It seems two billion miles from here, away from his merry horseshit, doing Spanish things; sipping sherry, reading news about America, just watching life be Spanish in Spain for a moment.

Emotionally, the idea of being somewhere else is a beautiful divorce, complete with a fantastic alimony.

Coming back ...

Lynn laughs a bit too much. Sometimes I suspect she is almost hysterical and it's hard to figure out why. Maybe she's having her period. I'm beginning to pay more attention to things like that.

Cute De-Lores (that's the way she's taught everyone to say it, "De-Lores") smiles hesitantly and keeps on doing her thang, whatever it is. Came into class yesterday looking like Brazilian Indian, with her hair cropped as though it had been cut under a soup bowl.

Incredibly interesting hairstyles the sisters have, simply incredible. Some of what they are and who they are finds definite expression through their hair shapings.

Rougenia, for example, slips us straight into Masai Land with her close napped cut, Rozetta (Rozita, Rossita, etc.) will uncover an old fashioned bunch of what used to be caled "plaits," Ovida stuns with intricate corn rows, and on and on. Some mornings it takes me fifteen minutes to admire the heads before I can begin to make my typing errors. The effect is more stimulating than two cups of caffeined coffee.

Speaking of hair, just discovered a young sister from Nigeria named Chindah, very nice to talk to. She sports a Farrah-Fawcett flip out. Oh well.

I see wounded, scarred women, staggering under emotional loads that would break an Olympic weightlifter's back but, somehow they carry on.

I trip across them, crying in odd corners, or staring off into the other side, too hurt to cry again.

There are no counterbalances, no "happiness" that makes their burdens lighter; they carry the weight and bitch, get high, act tough, sing, dance, eat too much, but the weight remains. They make me feel more like a man, to be sharing some of the load.

People are constantly surfacing with different stuff.

Carlotta LaBlanche has informed us that her real name *is* definitely Lotta B. Black. She said it, as usual, with a liquid laugh and a delicate little gesture. "You hear me?"

Now this; the Administration has discovered the dangers of "Self Paced" Learning and someone is trying to correct it, after fifteen weeks.

The Self Paced Learning Process was supposed to give us a chance to learn whatever we were supposed to be learning at our own speed. That was the problem.

It came to a head with me, when we were informed that we were going to be tested on material that our "self pacing" hadn't taken us to (I must've been up to kindergarten #101 in shorthand). I came out of the box and wrote a "No Final Exam" manifesto. Politics started happenin.

Other thangs be happenin . . .

It was the experience of watching these beautiful black women pollute themselves with junk food that made me do it.

I started a lunch hour exercise class; me, playing Master Kim to a small, hardcore, dyno group of Afrikan-American females who have the nerve and grit to work out at midday on a 99 degree afternoon. Hot.

We go slowly but surely toward a goal. They have Fire and I come to them coldbloodedly. We make interesting combinations happen.

I asked, one heat-crazed afternoon, for everyone to fast . . . for a day. They stared at me as though I had grown a tail.

The shorthand breakthrough happened for a moment, thanks to Delceen. She whispers the right things at the right times and suddenly it's there, the meaning of that weird slur on the page that I could never figure out.

Delceen has a twelve year old son who could be the next Mongo Santamaria. He plays with metronomic force and his imagination allows him to do things that many older drummers haven't thought about.

(I heard, saw him play at our school picnic.)

The exercise program broke down. We are all a bunch of hedonists. And lazy to boot. They couldn't make themselves believe that they were actually going to work up a sweat at lunch time.

Ovida: "Every day? You must be outta yo mind?"

Into the room the women come and go, talking about everything but Michelangelo.

Haven't seen Rougenia for a week, someone says she's doing something in Alabama.

"Wherever she is you know she doin somethin abstract."

Carol is missing too. No one has any idea where she is. But no one has any idea of where she came from either.

Rougenia returned, still talking "abstract." Despite this "abstract" label, the woman is a shorthand writin 'n readin wizard and she ain't too bad on the typewriter.

No one seems to be capable of explaining where her talent springs from.

"Rougenia? She abstract."

It's criminal that television is so white and blind; the sit-com that these sisters would make could keep America laughing and crying until the end of Time.

Olivia Williams' mother died today (July 18th, 1978).

Surprises continue, continue, continue. Cassandra and I had a lunch hour. That seems to happen, from time to time; I'll find myself with one of the sisters, seemingly without planning for that to happen.

There are times, however, when we do plan.

"Are we goin to have lunch together or not?"

Cassandra. Her grasp of the Amerikkan political situation, evaluated on her own terms, is tremendous.

That seems to be par for the course, scratch the surface and right there beneath the skin is a Power Source. Roylene is right, Melanin must be a power-intelligence source.

One still finds plenty of time to get high.

The weekend is here and I sit here with a Heineken dark, bringing myself good cheer.

Saturday, July 22, 1978: thinking about what life is about. Jan Baby shakes me awake after having dreamed of Death. I didn't know how to tell her that I saw her skeleton, the bones were black.

(Went up to Ivan Dixon's pad in Altadena to pick up my conga on this hot, hot afternoon. Good brother, Ivan Dixon, very complex.)

These sisters are so deep. The following is black women on black women. The quotes will not be identified, for obvious reasons. Years from now, I want to feel safe in my sleep.

"Y'all say Rougenia abstract, I say that broad is crazy. You hear me?"

"Wonda is one of the biggest, finest women I ever seen. I think it's got something to do with the way she dresses. Ain't too many big women know how to wrap material around they bodies so that it look good."

"I think Vicki is for real about her religion. When I see her readin her Bible I know it ain't for show. The sister is real."

"Valencia needs a man, bad."

"Where did she go?"

"Who?"

"What's her name?"

"I can never remember her name."

"You must be talkin 'bout Miss Thang Thang."

"I don't know about some of the sisters, they just get so far off the track sometimes. You know what I mean? With all this reefer smokin 'n stuff. I mean, what sense does it make to be doing shorthand, loaded?"

"I know I'm fine! I think I'm fine as anybody in the world. Look how black 'n shiny my skin is. Look at my ass! Look at my titties! Shit! Cain't nobody tell me I ain't fine."

"It don't matter what color a woman is. Black women is black and white women is white and yellow women is yellow. I don't know what color Mesican women is, some of 'em look red to me. But I know I'm black 'n that's a fact."

"I know they be sayin I talk abstract and what not, but what's that mean?"

"Now that's what *I* call a beautiful sistah."

"What makes her a beautiful sistah?"

"If you cain't see it, ain't no way I can explain it to you, honey."

"Black women are different. I don't know, there's just somethin about us. I don't know how to quite put it like, well, I've hung out with a bunch uh different kinda chicks. I was in jail, at one point, up in Minnesota with a whole bunch uh white girls'n everything was cool. I mean, like we didn't have a lot of race problems'n stuff.

"I think the thing I've noticed is that sistuhs is deeper. You know what I mean? Yeahhh, that's one of the differences. We

85

deeper ... "

Ovida, Marie, Anita, Gail, Charisse and I took another one of "those" lunch hours together. (July 26, 1978)

We sat out on the grass of the stadium at West Los Angeles City College, surreptitiously smoked a bit of the holy herb and rapped. Or rather, they rapped, I listened.

Marie, passionately: "I was fuckin a man for about three years who had a wonderful dick. I mean, it was wonderful."

Ovida: "Yeahhh, you come across one of them, every now'n then."

Gail: "What's so wonderful about some dude's dick?"

Marie: "You'll find out when you get one."

Charisse: "I don't see how y'all could sit round'n talk about this kind o' stuff with him around."

Ovida: "You ain't gon tell nobody 'bout this, is you sweet thang?"

Spacing back; most of the impressions I had, a while back, when it seemed that people were "cool," have to be revised. There are no "cool" women in the class.

There are moments when the steam rising from their bodies crates a sensual haze above our heads, a combination of menstrual funk, hormonal changes (somebody is always getting pregnant) Essence d'female noir and potato chips.

I can't think of any of them as lovers, specifically, physically. Well, five or six come to mind, but not forty-odd.

Sometimes I have an inkling of what the ladies in the Harem must go thru, waiting for the sheik to show up. In my case, I constitute a harem of one and I have forty sheiks, psychologically.

Sometime in the future I'd like to write a giant Valentine's Day poem to/for them, I'd call it "Sisters."

Damn! Missed school two days (July 27-28), hope I didn't miss anything.

I didn't; my soulschoolmates informed me that nothing unusual or spectacular had occurred. Same-o same-o somebody said.

August 6th, Sunday. Tripped out to Compton, to sing and dine with the Vernon's while Jan slept. I'll be glad when her horrible graveyard shift is over.

In any case, having slept in the afternoon, I find myself wide awake at 3:30 a.m., thinking, once again, about my classmates.

Ovida curls up in my brain, dances around, speaks to me through this chocolate coated veil, the way she speaks? I feel deeply about and for her.

Ovida loves me (at the moment) but I cannot help her. Strange feeling, to have a beautiful woman pursue you and know that she will never catch you.

I analyzed our situatin coldly, mercilessly. We would make tempestuous love for a few months, maybe a year, and it would be delicious. And then the rot would settle in.

We'd argue about me reading when she wanted to be out dancing.

Her world is not quiet, my world begs for quiet.

We would finally wind up hating each other because we shared a sphere that didn't belong to either of us, one that we couldn't share. I saw it, it flashed through the back of my brain like a video and it hurt. August 8th. Went to lunch with tall Gail (she had no money and felt bad about it), Ovida, Tina and Marie, names for future children. And smiles.

The food was pizza and the problem was the anchovies on it. Gail picked what she thought was a hair out of an anchovy body. And, despite the fact that it was her idea in the first place, Ovida rejected the whole fish, Tina ignored hers and smoked cigarettes and Marie got sick, thinking that she had eaten one. The sisters are not into "foreign" food.

Another day, another restaurant, a slightly more adventurous mix.

Rougenia, Carlotta La Blanche, Wonda the Wonder and, of course, Ovida.

"Where do you go for lunch?"

"I'm going down to this Cuban place?"

Ovida was beginning to affect my speech pattern.

"What kind of food do they have?"

"Chinese food?"

"Don't be funny, man. You're not going to another one of those places where they have that smelly fish, are you?"

"You ordered the anchovy pizza, remember?"

They invited themselves to accompany me. What could I do, complain?

Off we trip to La Cubana.

Really fine restaurant, La Cubana, unpretentious, honest, two cooks from deepest Mantanzas, dervishes with fish and chicken.

We scored five big points falling through the door. The sight of these four beautiful, down to earth African-American women from east of Main Street, loaded on pre-lunch herb and effervescence forced the most conversative Cuban woman in the place to smile .

Fortunately, it was slightly beyond the busy-busy-lunch time and they had the time to enjoy our show.

For story purposes, it should be stated up front that we had a beginning, a middle and an end, but all of what went on in between could never be covered by any manual of writing.

It took us fifteen minutes to decide where to sit. Wonda wanted, of course, to sit at a table in the center of the room, alone.

Carlotta couldn't see herself sitting with her back to the door. Ovida wanted "a good table" and Rougenia, losing interest, wandered off to talk with a couple flirtatious looking Cuban dudes in her version of Spanish.

"Versi compre me'all, huh?"

I forced everyone to accompany me to a table at the west wall, we'd be shot in the direction where the ocean flowed from.

Someone clicked Celia Cruz up a couple notches and their shoulders started dancing.

"What kinda place did you say this was?"

"Cuban."

"Shit! That bitch sound like 'Retha!"

"Really!"

The menu made the shoulders pause for a break point.

"Uhh ohhh, he done done it again. How the hell we 'spose to read this? It's in a foreign language."

"Look on the other side."

"Oh."

We argue over the possibility of anybody with any sense eating squid in ink, let alone ordering it.

"Squid? Ain't that the thang in horror movies that's always stranglin' people with all those arms?"

"Fried *bananas? Fried bananas?*"

"Please not so loud."

I ordered flan, dessert first, sweets all around. The waiter frowned but delivered. It took a little under the table wrasslin to persuade Carlotta to pour some of her Bacardi dark on each of the portions but she did, finally, and the battle was three fourths over.

"Mmmmmm . . . this is gooooood. You hear me? This *is* good!"

The restaurant released a collective sigh of relief and the feasting began.

"Black beans? I always wondered about that. I'm from down home and I never saw no black beans growing nowhere."

"Do they dye 'em?"

The waiter relayed the question to the manager who relayed the question to the cook who sent out an extra serving, seasoned to perfection. That was that.

The chicken and rice and the fish and shrimp and yes, the squid in ink was spread on the table with gracious smiles and advice.

"It will be much better if you don't use the salt. The chef, he has already seasoned it just right for you."

Fifteen, sixteen Coronas, Carta Blancas, Dos Equis, Bohemias later . . .

"Shit! Mexican food ain't never tasted this good, I'm gon make R.B. bring me here the next time we go out for dinner."

We pulled off a Bay of Pigs Invasion at least once a week after that, and did not have to retreat once.

I try, self-consciously, to make myself a revolving center, a multi-faceted performer. Sometimes it works, sometimes it doesn't.

Vicki Adams and I have a thang goin on. We touch right hands every morning, not one of those jock slaps at "high noon" but a serious, firm, palm to palm touch.

Good flows from her. I feel it. I don't know what she gets from me.

We got a heavy jolt watching the regular students return for fall registration. They seemed like members from another society.

We've had the campus to ourselves all summer and now these, these *other* people show up. You could almost feel a kind of hostility surfacing.

"Where in the fuck was they at when it was hot?"

Aside, again: How do these ladies manage to smoke all this dope and concentrate? Got to be strong minded people up in here: strongminded, fiercely clever, timid, vulnerable.

Their emotions rocket from one plane to another; today someone is flat broke, the next day rich, in love, evicted, pregnant, high, had an abortion, depressed, elated or in states between.

There is a strong hyperthing going on all the time. It definitely has something to do with the food they eat.

I could do a book on the subject of their dietary jujitsuing. It would be a terrible book because they eat terribly.

Some of the concoctions are store bought (the queasy french fries, popcorn, pork rinds—"skins"—twinkies, etc.) and some of it is home made, the sugar on white bread sandwiches, for example.

And in the middle of this nutritional tragedy, beautiful skins, bodies and teeth surface. Maybe some of their intestines have developed the capacity to convert crap into art. Who can say?

Flash! Or maybe Flicker!

The strong possibility of this program not completing its cycle is borne out by low attendance figures and the pictures of the instructors surreptitiously scanning the want ads.

I'm at several crossroads . . .

A) A book is being ground thru the Saxton-Harper Grant˚ Mill, $10,000 at stake here and publication. Will it be *Harlem Blues* in 1979?

B) A reading of "memories of Momma" at Udwiis' and the possibility of creating a hip "little theatre."

C) Haven't heard from R'wanda Lewis yet. Will they grant me the funds to do a dance book?

D) Stanley Robertson has "Willis D. Jenkins" at Universal. Will they buy it? ("She's Gotta Have It" and "Hollywood Shuffle" (1986-87) have opened a few minds, maybe I'll try it again, tomorrow).

E) Will it be necessary to spend my declining years in the U.S. Post Office? What will the Deal be. Help! Somebody! August 20, '78 (it's '87. Now, is that prophetic or what?) Help! Jan, waking up from a nap, feeling bitchy about going to work (who wouldn't feel bitchy goin to Children's Hospital at 11:30 at night, to duly record the perverse behaviors of Los Angelenos. ("Baby Jane," 8 months old, raped by father.)

August 20/78

Felton called this evening to inform us that he will be coming thru the first week in September. The Chicagoans are trying to get a warmup before the Hawk whips in.

August 28th 1978.

One of the ladies in the class. In the simplest terms expressionable, I got bent out of shape today, at the tailend of a hot, dreary, mind boggling day, by a sister named Tina.

Tina is one of the sisters I've lunched with, rapped with, been friendly with. I don't really know what provoked her mindless display of hostility toward me but, suddenly, it was happening.

As I strolled past her (I resisted playing cock o' the walk altogether) she flicked a burning match onto my chest.

"Hey! Tina! Watch that! You might burn somebody!"

I pause, trying to make light (no pun, really) of the situation, she flicks another one on me. And another one. She may as well have spat on me. That was the effect it had on my psyche.

I stepped out ofher match throwing range and thought the business over quickly, carefully. It was a no-win situation for me. If I kicked her ass all over the campus, I'd just be another dog ass nigger showing off his macho.

If I allowed her to burn me up I'd lost my temper, literally.

I walked away from her and felt like a real black belt, level 8. I never did find out what provoked her.

Other developments. Miss Douglas, the only really white woman (Anglo S.P.) left in the class (if we excuse swarthy "white" Desiree and Ashkenazaic Jewish Lady Speigel) still laughs a wee bit too hysterically at times, but the laugh is no longer manic.

We've become guarded friends. I say, "guarded" because the sisters surround me and want me to be theirs only. I fight a feeble battle for independence.

And one day, as suddenly as it started, it came to an end.

The ending was truly anti-climatic. The Haley-Lear collaboration (Tandem Productions) offered me an opportunity to write a show ("Old Sister") for the *Palmerstown* series (it lasted six (6) shows) and the program cut me loose because I had too many unexcused absences.

It was cool. I was cool.

We separated, but never divorced (the marriage was designed in Heaven and destined to remain valid as long as Hell is reputed to be hot) me and the sisters in the program.

From time to time, they resurface, in single file, in single file, individually . . .

"Wowww! You mean you have money to put in the bank?"

"And you're a bank teller?"

"Yes, I am?"

Chapter 4

Tough Titty '87: A Dark Collage

In The Beginning Were The Words ... "Look June, See Spot Run."

Fattenin' Frogs For Snakes

"How you like it, baby?"

"It's really nice, Milfred ... really nice. How much are they chargin' us for the place?"

"Four hundred'n fifty a month."

"That ain't bad ... and it's really roomy too."

Ella strolled slowly across the highly polished wooden floor, enchanted by the spaciousness of the room.

Milfred watched every move, high already from being up all night polishing the floor and smoking three joints.

High on Ella . . . in love. Was she going to move in or not? And with two crumbcrushers, still the finest looking, lil' ol' halfass exotic, New Orleans born black woman in town. Wowwwww!

"Milfred, I think we oughta hurry up and get some rugs on the floor, don't you?"

"Uh huh."

"Goddamnit! Ella! I get off at two, I get home at 2:30 . . . at 3, I wanna be smackin my jaws together on somethin tasty . . . don't make no sense to be livin with a woman who can't have your meals on time! Shit!"

Mobile Fornication, Tri-Sexually

"It was funniest of all when we stopped at red lights, I mean, like you could hear things in a way you've never heard before. Imagine what it would sound like, there we were, in the fold out bed in the camper, Lorenzo is drivin and Phillip and myself are closed up in back, fuckin like two sex starved Russian gorillas.

Everytime we'd almost get up to it, what with the camper bouncin us up'n down, into all kinds a crazy rhythms . . . anyway, just as we'd be about to cum together, or try to . . . Lorenzo would jam up to a light or swerve around a corner.

Those corners! Goddamn! Phillip would be about to slide away off me and I'd have to lock my legs around his waist to hold him in.

I don't think I need to tell you that all three of us was loaded to the jibbs. Lorenzo had dropped about six reds and between us we must've smoked about eight joints, *and* we had some Red Mountain.

After about a half hour, I forget where we was 'sposed to

96

be goin. Lorenzo stopped the camper, lifted the curtain and asked . . . oh so politely, if we could switch up cause he was tired a drivin.

We all cracked up because the situation was so . . . uhhh, hip. Yeahhh, hip is the word. The way he put it and everythang.

He knew that only one of us was climbin out of the rack, and he didn't really give a damn cause . . . cause . . . he didn't really give a damn.

Phillip made things real simple by puttin on his clothes and crawling down into the driver's seat.

Lorenzo was pullin his pants down over the biggest hard on I'd seen when this cop opened the door and asked us, "What the hell's goin on in here? Why're you people parked on the railroad tracks?"

Tryin' Times

"Now then, Mr. DuBois . . . that's an unusual name, French, isn't it?"

"Uhh huhn."

"Yes, well, ahhemm, to get back to where we were. Your application is, I must say, extraordinarily neat. You know, most of the fellows coming in to apply for a position do not have the slightest notion of the kind of impression they make with their applications. Yes, yours is just fine, just fine."

"Thank you."

Ms. H. Thaddeus Sternum flashed a glossy, goddness-gracious-you're-a-nice-guy-smile on brother man Hugo DuBois and eased away from her desk with a curt "excuse me a sec" to check the employment agency's bad guy file, to make certain this nice DuBois wasn't another DuBois, a nasty DuBois from some other time.

Brother man DuBois slouched slightly, watching Ms. Sternum's flat buttocks twitch behind a set of filing cabinets.

Bitch is goin to check on me, bigger'n shit!

He tried to place a detached, unconcerned expression on his face as his eyes wandered coldly from one desk to another.

Another office, the same people, all of them working toward the coffee break, a newer car, more money . . . Somethin' . . . and all I want is a job.

Ms. Sternum returned to her desk with the same superbright expression she always wore when she felt she was dealing with a reasonably intelligent applicant.

"Mr. DuBois," she began hesitantly, "we only have two openings, both of which I will have to veto for you."

"Huh?"

"Well, the first opening is with the County Custodial Services Department, a janitor, in other words . . . "

"What's the other one?"

"Stock . . . uhhh . . . clerk, in one of the downtown department stores."

"Which one pays the most ?"

"Well, the Custodial Services Department does, in addition to offering civil services benefits."

"Good, I'll take that one."

Ms. Sternum looked past Hugo DuBois' head at the clock, fifteen minutes before the break.

"Mr. DuBois, may I speak frankly, confidentially?" she asked him in a low, classy voice.

"Yeah, why not."

"Mr. DuBois, you've had a year of junior college, you've—"

"Yeah, but I'm forty eight years old and next year I'll be forty nine and I needs a steady gig rightin through here."

Ms. Sternum felt the sphincter tighten in her rectum as she committed herself to the only decision she felt possible to make. Damn these hemorrhoids!

"Mr. DuBois, I must apologize for an oversight, I've just notfied that the two positions *were* available. They were filled yesterday. I'm terribly sorry ... "

Brother Hugo stared at Ms. Sternum's glistening forehead and resisted the urge to fire on her, got up slowly and shuffled out of the office, holding back rage.

Ms. Sternum stared at his back briefly and then began to shuffle some pages around on her desk.

Attractive, well spoken man ... appears to be a really decent type. He'll find something better than a janitor's job or working as a stockboy.

God! how much longer will it be before lunch?

Holiday In The Projects

Blam slam scratch fight fuck how many babies are too many for the space allotted?

Monday music a lil' less loud than Saturday music what difference does it make?

You know despair? Yeah, she lives on the sixth floor right underneath Sister Anguish an' both of'em be fuckin everybody.

Throw it out the motherfuckin window 'sposin it hits somebody?

So?

Suck on us motherfuckers suck it all out but be sure and leave some throats and lungs for the smoke some arms for the fires some skulls for barbequeing.

Drums children babies mothers beautiful sisters—like heyyy—I mean beautiful beautiful women not commercially beautiful like black is beautiful but beautiful uniquely.

Pregnant women with babies larger than anybody's mind pregnant mind with minds larger than the women's bellies but no place to give birth stagnated plunged into concrete ghosts.

Old ladies thirty four years old old; old mothers deliriums. His-story in concrete this time, the Indian safely chewed up on the reservation.

Catastrophes all mellowed out cooled cooled down by bad wine in black back pockets readily reachable.

Joint in jibbs and just in case if all else fails, sweet heroin.

Holiday in the projects a trip not advertised in the travel folders and offices.

But what the fuck do they know about a real trip?

Big Sister And The Trick

"Big Sister! Big Sister! tell Charleston to gimme my quarter back! I had it layin on the dresser'n he took it! tell'im to give it back."

"Awwwww, I ain't got no quarter o' hers! She's tellin a story!"

"Charleston! You know better than to be takin what don't belong to you, now give Leona her quarter back! now!"

"This ain't her quarter, Ella Jean! This is mine. I cashed some pop bottles in for this!"

"Awright, I tell you what, give it to me, that'll settle that!"

"But it's mine, Ella Jean! It's mine! I'm gon' tell Momma on you, goin 'round takin money from peoples."

"Boy! Gimme that quarter! I don't care what you tell Momma! Give it to me!"

Charleston Johnson, middle brother of a quartet of brothers sullenly, reluctantly handed over the stolen quarter, a quarter stolen from his sister, fuming.

"And don't be takin anything else that don't belong to you, o.k.?"

Charleston nodded solemnly, put down, pissed off. Leona smiled, knowing her money was in good hands.

"Big Sister," Ella Jean Johnson, fourteen years old and substitute mother for the seven member clan, took the quarter and pushed it down into the pocket of her blue jeans, disgusted.

She looked meanly at Charleston, implying that she was just about two seconds off of his ass, and that he could tell Momma whenever she showed up.

Momma Johnson, gone two days now, off, away in desperation, tired of being somebody's Momma, seeking some temporary happiness in whatever form he happened to occur in.

Charleston glared back, briefly, aware that Ella Jean, with her notoriously bad temper, might jump on him. She looked away from Charleston's hostile face, around at her sisters and brothers and felt helpless, small, childish.

"Big Sister," an unearned position, with absolutely no commission. No time to break down, to give up ...

"Marvin, you and Rosalee, y'all better to wash out somethin to wear to school tomorrow. Charleston, since you so busy stealin, have you done your homework yet?"

Charleston jammed his hands down into pockets stuffed with scraps, tidbits and bit ends of a day spent roaming the streets, instead of going to school and nodded softly, no. Not wanting to admit that he never had homework to do, even when he went to school.

"Well, you better git on your job then!"

Assigning things to be done, giving some kind of direction, needing some, bored and disturbed by too much responsibility, wanting to take a break ... maybe I can find Momma, I know where she might be.

"Listen y'all, I got to run down to Melba's for a few minutes, don't tear up the house while I'm gone. And don't nobody go out, it's too late and besides, ain't nobody out there but thugs anyway. That goes for you too, Marvin!"

"Awwwwww, Ella, why you have to stay on my case all the time? I wasn't even thinkin 'bout goin nowhere," he replied, annoyed that she should have guessed that he was planning to sneak out.

"You heard what I said!" she grated each word out at him.

After making certain that Rumboy, the four year old, was curled up with his toy horse, left thumb securely in his mouth, she eased out of the door, stood with her ear pressed to it for a moment, listening for the chaos she knew would erupt the minute she was out of sight.

Quietly letting herself back in, she grabbed the first wrongdoer she could get her hands on, Leona teasing Charleston, and swacked her on the behind five hard times.

"I told you 'bout that, didn't I, Leona? Didn't I?"

Leona smeared a stream of I-been-treated-wrong-tears across the bridge of her nose and nodded solemnly, "uhhhn huhhhn."

"Now that goes for all the rest of you all. Finish doin what you got to do and carry your asses to bed! I'll be back in a lil' while."

Everyone, including Marvin, the would be escapee, cowed by Ella Jean's foresight and power, set about the work they had to perform with renewed energy.

She made a bold exit this time, confident that everything would be all right.

Closing the door she didn't bother to listen back, knowing from experience that her show of force had been enough.

She smiled slightly walking slowly down the garbage scattered stairs from their tenth floor apartment in the projects.

Too bad, she thought, my brothers'n sisters won't really pay me any mind 'til I have to snatch one of 'em.

She almost stepped on the rat's tail before she realized it and he, making hostile squeaks, waddled, first into one corner, panicking, confused, and then along the wall facing the steps.

Ella Jean hurriedly backed up a few steps to give him room, afraid of being bitten.

It looked vaguely, in the dim light, with the scar tissue ridging its back, like Ol' Tom, a fierce old guy who had refused poisoned food, evaded traps and had a taste for baby flesh. "Goes for the milk smell," someone said, after five had been bitten, one in the groin, but she didn't feel certain, as she watched him tumble down the next level of steps and through a hole in the concrete wall.

Fuckin rats!

She continued down the stairs, cautiously checking out the shadowed corners, for whatever might be lurking there.

The seventh floor, Marshmellow and four members of his gang, the Trojan Pimps, gettin high.

"Heyyyy, where you on your way, lil' sister?"

Ella Jean felt the urge to scream at Marshmellow, "Bigggg Sister, motherfuckaahhhh! Bigggg Sister! Goddamn you!" Instead, stoically, she made her way past their sly whispers, wishing they wouldn't be smokin'n drinkin so much.

Especially Marshmellow, good looking dude, only seventeen and always loaded. And Darnell, and Freddie Bob, and Maxwell and . . .

She dropped the thought, past them and their suggestions now, concentrating on where it might be possible to find her mother.

How did that poem go? The one Mrs. MacRae had read them, by Imanu Baraka . . . "Calling all black people, calling all black people . . . "

Callin my momma, she thought bitterly, callin my momma . . . come in, momma, wherever you are . . . and not just because we're all out of milk, break, money and love either.

Where in the hell could she be?

Starting from her usual point, she walked north on Wabash Avenue, to 61st Street, turned the east corner on 61st and strolled along the south side of the street, peering into the windows of various joints she suspected her mother might be in.

A man she had found her mother drinking with, in the All Fun Inn, weeks ago, laughed in his beer mug at her question.

"Nawww, babysweets . . . hahhahhahhahhaha, I ain't seen yo momma, not this week anyway, last time I seen'er, she beat me outta ten dollars."

Feelin numb on the humid, lonely streets turning south at 61st and Cottage Grove, and then turning west on 63rd Street, the roar of the El trains above her, Ella Jean felt like crying.

Crying or fighting was the way her brothers and sisters seemed to be able to take care of their problems. No way to solve the need but that's what they did.

She struggled for tears, staring at bright street lights, hoping to bleed tears from staring at the lights, but they refused to come.

Where in hell could she be? She'd be back home in the next couple days, the check being due on the 15th, maybe before . . . but how would that give them more than more red beans'n rice, black eyed peas'n hocks, neck bones or grits and sugar?

Ella Jean stared into the window of a suspected joint, cupping her hands around her eyes in the neon glare of the front, both inside and out, hoping that her mother would be inside.

Fancy sisters and Superflown brothers circulated their most blase looks out at her, amused by the sight of the innocent brown face pressed against the glass.

Satisfied that she wasn't there, she walked on, enjoying the barbequed fragrances of the Southside's deep summer air, in spite of the heavy feelings she carried with her.

Digging down in her jeans, she felt Leona's quarter and

almost laughed aloud.

Wowwwww! I got coins.

What could you do with a quarter?

She thought seriously about it, crossing three streets that led back to Wabash Avenue, her street, the projects.

What could you do with a quarter? You sho' as hell couldn't buy enough of anything to feed seven people, you couldn't pay the rent . . .

What the fuck!

She stopped in the neighborhood shrimp house and bought a coke for twenty cents, smiled the gentle giant-owner of the place out of a handful of cellophaned saltines, stole a mini-pac of catsup and continued on her way, back home. Best thing to do is wait for momma, if she ain't in the neighborhood, no tellin where she might be.

The man calling to her from the car, and the color of him surprised her.

A cop?

"Hay girlie, c'mere!" he called to her, looking around anxiously as his car slid up beside her at the curb. "You wanna make twenny bucks? Huh? How 'bout it?" he asked again, a panic-striken expression on his lined, grey, middle-aged face.

She stared at him neutrally, analytically. Middle-aged white dude, frightened shitless about being on the southside after dark, looking for black meat . . . a trick! Yeahh! A tremblin white trick.

She saw the pop bottle splatter against the side of his car before she fully realized she had thrown it.

The white man bared his teeth at her like an animal for a moment, his anger almost driving him out at her before he remembered where he was.

"Why you little dirty black bitch!" he screamed at her and gunned away from the curb.

Ella Jean watched the car's lights disappear around the next corner before she resumed her walk home, crying, but not really knowing why.

From New York, And Other Strange Places

Harlem, a windswept, fish fried cry in a desert of white numbness . . .

Harlem, a smoke-turned, barbecued rib with scars on its face, nibbled on by white rats in 5th Avenue penthouses . . .

Harlem, a cold, clean shot of muddy heroin in the eyeball . . . a salute to the goodwill of Our Lady Mafia.

Harlem, sponsored by the vomit from the stomach pits of vultures and needle nosed sharks, positioned into place by trips to the moon and sophisticated white racism.

Harlem, a lustrous dark face in a wide window, breasts filled with milk so black, so rich that a drop of it in the President's coffee would kill him.

Harlem, white lips on a sculptured brown face, green eyes in a cocoa colored one, red eyes everywhere . . .

Harlem, Johannesberg, Sharpeville, America's contribution to the final black solution, sightseeing buses through what the racists have developed as an institution . . .

Harlem, hip, slick, cool, down . . . in, out, wowww! yeahhh! really! dig! uhhhn huhhhh . . . bayyy-beee, right on!

Harlem, after stopping, being able to go another fu'ther, goin right on!

Harlem . . . home.

Brother Mannnnn . . .

"Yeahhh, so there I was, you dig . . . on the University

of Oregon campus, don't ask me how I got there . . . waitin!
I knew if I sat in one spot long enough somebody was, somethin would put in an appearance that would save me, you dig,
some somethin! Yeahhh, and sho' nuff it did, or rather I
should say, she did . . . uhh huh. Sho' did. Showed up outta
the fog like a bee-nevolent spirit, folded me up into her luscious white arms and carried me away like a baby . . . like
a nachul bone baby . . . uhhhuh, that's right, sho' did.

My game was tighter than Dick's hatband, knew she was
into somethin 'cause she was dealin from a white Mercedes,
had to be into somethin, yeahhh, really.

Stylish, middle-aged bitch, had been everywhere'n done
everything, you hear me, brother mannnnn? everything!!
Yeahhh, uhhh huh, ever'thang!

Awwww, it was beautiful, you dig, really beautiful, while
it lasted.

I was rippin, slippin'n slidin through the streets of Port-
land like a black shadow, pockets stufed fulla dough, so many
pretty clothes on my back that it would take me an hour,
sometimes, to undress . . . yesssuh, that's the honest to God's
truth . . . uh huh. Whatchu gon do? You gon cut out on me,
brother mannnn, rightin through here?

Yeahhh, uhh huh, o.k. then, be that way . . . but looka here,
'fore you git on, why don't you let me hold one o' them quar-
ters you got stuck of down in yo' pocket, so I can get somethin to steady my nerves with?"

That Village Scene, That Village Thing . . .

Chinese Fellinis in Gloria Steinhem hairstyles,
Cartoon pantleggings from Moon Mullins and Lil' Orphan
Annie . . .
Black girls strolling hand in hand with their Jewish boy-

friends, a new kibbutzim for tired African hearts.

Hair hair everywhere and sitting behind some of it in a movie theatre is enough to make one ask . . . "What's goin on?"

Black dudes, brothers, with translucent zippers, spinning their tricky pricks around in effervescent pink shorts . . . swollen up by punk pussy.

Engorged Puerto Rican sweethearts, eyes watering from the cold, squeezing frozen fruit and wondering, what happened to the sun?

Hindus with luscious, eclectic minds trickling elephant vowels from frosted mustaches, searching for Khrisna and Kleenex . . .

Jews, Holy men with fetlocks Shirley Templed from Talmudic heads, New York Jet fans.

Dazzling, glistening, gooey gobs of books, welded, wedded together by category and title.

The Village Voice, the so-called radical's choice, you don't have to be Swedish to love our bread.

Spilling, spinning, spooling, spooning . . . splittin . . . damn the Automats.

Just Greens'n Things

Just gimme good greens'n things . . . or hoghead cheese, butter beans'n Momma's black eyed peas . . . don't serve no Mandarin duck or marshmellow stew here please . . .

Just gimme some greens'n things . . . collards, turnips, spinach'n mustard topped by a meaty hock . . . hot water cornbread to lick the pot likker up . . . no fancy Russian fish eggs, moldy cheese'n funny crackers served here please . . .

Just gimme some greens'n things . . .

Just lay some greens'n things on me . . . !

Brains'n eggs when my feet first hit the floor, grits'n stuff to hold me 'til you finish the red beans'n rice, or good gumbo file fixed the way girls from Louisiana used to do . . .

Or just plain ol' greens'n things.

Trip me out if you want to on tripe, egg batter fried chicken'n honey flavored biscuits, made from scratch, stewed Arkansas squirrel, Louisiana froglegs and west Texas rabbits . . . or . . . if you can't manage that, just stick some grees'n things to me . . . Smothered steak, navy beans, pole beans, neck bones'n cabbage, cool red tomatoes and candied sweet potatoes . . . mountain oysters . . . uhh huh . . . oxtails, peach cobblers'n mellow bread puddin's . . .

Or just plain ol' greens'n things . . . Git on down to the pig if you have to . . . Pig snout'n po'k sausage, hog maws'n funky chitlins . . . chops from the side'n Virginia ham . . . but if you ain't got none o' that . . .

Please . . . just gimme some greens'n things . . .

Blacknest Up In Here . . .

Zulu men, old fathers, young brothers, left handed women with white livers on the fringes of the fire . . .

The blaze shooting up out of an oil drum, nursed in the cold by the warmth around it . . .

Twenty dark tales and fifty black Afro-verbs jostling each other . . . splitting off into the shadows, climbing up the walls of tenement huts around, beyond the First . . .

The wine bottle passed from lip to lip, bypassing them that hadn't put in . . .

The groaning of a two by four as it settled down comfortably into the bottom of the barrel.

Our grandest grandfather's face, seamed by lines that go back to the First Fire, stare past the flame, back into *his* father's eyes . . .

Ashy hands wave out calmly at the fire . . . warming calluses so old and hard that they look like gloves of stone . . .

Bottle goes back'round, counterclockwise, bypassing them that didn't put in.

Rugged sleeves smear themselves across runny noses, a quickly frozen glaze in the eastern cold.

Men, blackmen, tribesmen from many nations, gleam in the sudden glare of fifteen *New York Times* dumped in the barrel . . . Zulu there, with the smoldering eyes, Ga there, Dagga over there, a Kikuyu there, a cold, calm Masai there, Falasha here, Dogon there, the Great Lord Chaka strolling away, his back steaming.

Fire eases down, faces, bodies, spirits drawn in closer, heat slipping away . . . but not the warmth . . .

"Y'all wanna put in on another one?"

Brothers Be Zigzaggin Sometimes . . .

Brothers be zigzaggin sometimes . . .

Yeah, bruh, that's right, that's what I said, brothers be zigzaggin some times . . .

Like, I mean, when your woman be comin from somewhere, all by her sweet black self and gits stomped, raped, robbed *and* cut by nugguhhs . . .

Like, I mean, it might've been even worse for you 'cause they would've had to *really* jack you up, after all, she was just a po defenseless black woman.

Yeahhh, bruh . . . brothers be zigzaggin sometimes, brothers be zigzaggin when ain't but two bloods standin in the alley, drinkin rotgut pluck, and one, or the other, is tryin to figure out a way to fuck the other one up.

Uhhh huhh, that's right, brothers be zigzaggin lots times,

but lots o' people don't wanna talk about it.

Like, I mean, when black grandmothers with arthritis fear dim hallways because of spooks ...

When young brothers find theyselves afraid to show some smarts 'cause the dudes they hang out with say, "be cool ..."

When "stone love" makes corners bloody and innocent people suffer ...

Yessuh, bruh ... brothers be zigzaggin sometimes, I mean, like, dig this ...

I tripped down to the corner liquor store the other evenin, you know, just for a lil' taste to take me through the midnight hours.

I had just copped, was easin out and blam! the next thing I knew, three young brothers was on my case, like, I mean, that quick!

I hadn't done shit, hadn't said shit, been into nothin with them except misery shared on common ground, that's America I'm talkin 'bout.

Anyway, to make a long story short, I was forced to defend myself from the brothers! Can you git ready for that?

I was forced to defend myself from the brothers.

I mean, like, I had no idea to rap about my Tinley Park drug rehabilitation thang, or my summer camp work, or my art work, or any other fuckin kind of work ... no time to say coolly, rationally: "Hey, y'all know this don't make a bitta' sense!"

Cause the next thing I knew, scared as I was, I had punched one of 'em in the nuts with a half ass karate kick, fired a right dead to the other one's jaw and tryin to keep the third one from knockin my damned head off.

To tell the truth, I woulda ran, if I had had a chance, but they didn't gimme that, so we had to thump ...

Yeahhh, ain't that sad? Some really sick shit ... but, what can you say? That's the kind of shit that goes down when brothers be zigzaggin. Sometimes.

Postscript to Laura

It is now 12:15 p.m. and I'm laying here in my rack, thinking of how much I miss you. I don't believe it will ever be possible to flood your senses with the kind of longing I have for you, for your eyes, the dimples around your mouth, the rhythmic pattern of your stomach against mine.

I write a few words and then I have to lay back and cool myself out, the strength of the memory of the taste of your tongue fighting mine, the endless battles we fought that way, is enough to make me weak.

It will never be possible for me to let you know of my thirst for you now. I'll be twenty eight when I get out, if everything goes o.k., and during the course of all that time I won't be able to lean over your shoulder in the middle of the night and say: "Baby . . . baby, you sleep?"

My sweet black Laura . . . my little buck teethed Laura, my big fine Laura. Laura with the sad dark eyes, and delicious little dimples placed, ever so carefully, in the sweetest sections of your lower back.

I throb for you now, Laura . . . ebony globes of glistening jissum ooze out of my body, (please let this go through, Mr. Censorman) I have no control over the beautiful songs the thought of you causes my body to sing.

Please say to me in your return letter that you know, that you understand exactly how I feel right now.

I lay here and imagine that we are joined, linked across the miles in our thinking . . .

I must stop now, it's late and I mustn't make myself suffer for you. I'll be bitter if that happens and I don't want that to happen . . . I want to be sweet when we get it together again (smile)

Love, Always
Ronald

p.s.

Baby, I couldn't sleep. I tried and it wouldn't work. I was never aware that my body could feel the kind of heat within itself, that I feel right now, and not melt.

It seems as though I am outside myself, watching me lay here, face down on my narrow bunk, your face spilling over my pillow like a soft, warm shadow.

I'm dreaming now, I guess, my body fading in and out of you, your knees doubled up under my armpits, perspiration and excitement rolling down the sides of our bodies like warm ocean waves.

The motion changes, the record changes . . . you asked me to roll another joint, I asked you to get the Akadama out of the refrigerator.

We smoked and drank, nursing our mouths on each other's nipples, pushing the heavy, well-flavored smoke from one mouth to the other, spilling droplets of wine into each other's navels, and finally, after long minutes of stumbling around in nature's mental graveyard, we slithered back into each other's arms.

My extended, love hard muscle wedging itself into your tender pelvic petals, each of us joined to each other in a way that was not me in you, or you in me, but us in each other.

And now I wake up, fight away a feeling that is so unspeakably delicious that the waste of the feeling, the soft, creamy stickiness, causes me to cry, to hurt inside at the thought of so many more beautiful little black babies wasted.

And now the dream is over. I've sang to you 'til the grey prison light has lifted its ugly head over the wall again. Another day in the joint, but at least today, because I've shared this feeling, had a hard on, made my heart sing a little, drop-

ped my guard and declared my Love ... at least, because
of that, I won't have to stare at one of these ruby lipped punks
down in the yard and think of anything serious.

Love, again, always
Ronald

All Goodbyes Don't Mean Goodnight

"The Lawwwd works in mysterious ways!"

"God don't love ugly ... "

"A hard head makes a soft ass."

"Yo eyes may shine'n your teeth may grit, but none of this
shall you git."

"Ain't got a pot to piss in or a window to throw it out of."

"God takes care of fools, babies and drunks ... "

"Cold as a witch's left titty at midnight."

"Only a fool has to be told that fat meat is greasy."

Tight Jaws, A Domestic Scene

"And I guess you gon try to tell me y'all ain't fuckin every
chance you git? Huhn? Wake up goddamnit! Don't try to pretend you sleep, nigger!"

"Awwwww damn, woman! why don't you shut up'n go to
sleep?"

"I ain't goin to sleep, and you ain't neither! Not 'til we git
some kinda understandin, not 'til you tell me the truth about
you and that bitch! Y'all ain't been foolin nobody! I been
watching you two for a good lil while now. I don't know who
you think you foolin but you sho ain't foolin me, goddamn
you would-be tryin-to-be slick ass. The other day, when we
was walkin down to the supermarket, don't turn yo back on

114

me, Caesar Jones! You gon hear what I got to say, whether you like it or not!"

"Shirley! Goddamnit! Why don't you go to sleep so a man can get some rest, you know I got to get up early in the mornin and all this jawjackin ain't helpin matters at all, not worth a goddamn!"

"You got to git up! What about me? I got to git up too! But we got to git this shit straightened out first! I ain't nobody's fool, Caesar Jones! You best understand that now! and if you mean to try t'keep on tryin to put some shit in the game, I wants you to know, it ain't goin down here! By no means! I told you when we first moved into this place that we was gon play it straight or . . . wake up damnit! You ain't that sleepy!"

"Shirley, I don tol you! Hey! Don't be pullin the covers off me, it's cold!"

"You damned skippy it's cold! and it's gon be a whole lot colder if you don't tell me the truth!"

"If this ain't a bitch, I'll hush! What the fuck's the problem? What do you wanna know?"

"Very simple! I'm askin you straight out. Are you havin somethin t'do with that slant eyed heifer downstairs or not?"

"Awright, I'm tellin you for the last time . . . no! Capital N-capital-O! NO! Now lemme get some sleep, will you pleez? Pull the cover back up and act like somebody with some sense 'fore I lose *my* temper!"

"You lyin, Caesar Jones! You lyin yo rusty ass off! My girlfriend saw y'all goin into the Maryland the other day!"

"Which girlfriend? Who?"

"That's awright about which one! She saw you and she tol me what that cow had on and how you had your arm around her waist'n everything. Now I tell you what I'm gon do and I thought I'd let you know so you could get ready for it . . . I'm goin downstairs, first thing in the mornin, and if I don't

115

get the right answers to some of my questions, I'm gonna snatch that bean eyed bitch's head off!"

"Now just hold on, Shirley! Hold on a minute, baby. I don't think that that would be right at all. If you believe everything Carolynne tells ... "

"Carolynne! How did you know it was Carolynne? I didn't say it was Carolynne that saw you, but she *did* say you saw her while you was slippin'n slidin ... "

"Well ... uhh ruhh ... I ... uhh ... "

"See there! See how you lie! You lie faster than a cat can lick ass and you get worse all the time. I knew when I was movin in here with yo lyin ass that I was askin for trouble."

"Awwwww babyeee ... "

"Don't awwww babyeee me! And keep your hands to yourself! You 'bout fulla shit as a Christmas turkey! I've had all your bullshit I can stand when you come in tomorrow you can move that slit eyed wench right on in here 'cause I'll be gone. You hear me, Caesar Jones? Wake up! Don't be tryin to pretend you sleep! Caesar! Caesar! You hear me?"

Chapter 5
Writer's Block

Randolph Alexander, Black Writer, Another Victim

1. Exterior—MCM Studios—Day

Randolph Alexander, self understood poet, multifaceted prose singer, survivor of one thousand writing workshops, three hundred seminars on Black Authors, diligent reader of six hundred and eighty three books on "how to write a book," patient student of what it takes to shake good prose from a page, dedicated ear to all honest critiques of his work, a currently enrolled boot in the "cracked door" program, and a good, all around dude, stood in front of the entrance to the Marvin Stillberg building ... mind churning with the thought of earning grand theft dough writing a movie script that dealt with relevant issues of the day.

2. Interior—MCM—Day

Randolph is intercepted by a guard, put through a verbal frisk and hung up by two subconsciously white, racist receptionists ... demonstrating, evidently, that the producer who scheduled their meeting neglected to inform someone that Randolph would be dropping through.

1st Receptionist (cold, blue eyed, snotty bitch):
"Yesss, what can I do for *you*?

Randolph Alexander (super correct English):
"Ahhem, I'm here to see Mr. Blahwee Dowhee."

1st Receptionist (skeptically):
"Ohh. I see. Well, please be seated over there. I'll see if he's available."

Randolph sits, slightly nervous, holding onto his thriftshop briefcase, yellow legal pad and #2 pencils inside.

Receptionist talks to someone, somewhere, making it a point to reassure the party of the second part that she has absolutely no reason to even suspect what Randolph Alexander, black writer, is doing on the premises.

Receptionist #2 (strolling out of the inner sanctum, straightening her skirt, another snotty bitch):
"Mr. Alexander?"

Randolph (super sharp, crisply):
"Yes?"

Receptionist #2 (disdainfully):
"Will you come with me, please? Mr. Doowhee is expecting you and he hates to be kept waiting."

3. Inner Sanctum—Interior—MCM—Day

Elaborate, expensive furnishing. And at the other end of the ten inched pile of wall-to-wall Angora rug, seated grandly behind a huge, carved walnut desk, sits Mr. Blahwee Doowhee, Producer.

Receptionist #2:

"Mr. Doowhee? Mr. . . . uhh . . . Mr.?"

Randolph Alexander (modestly):

"Randolph Alexander."

Receptionist #2:

"Yes, Mr. Alexander is here to see you."

Mr. Blahwee Doowhee, his ears attached to two of the six telephones on his desk, motions impatiently with his cigar in his mouth for Randolph to come forth.

Randolph safaris through the rug pile, stands straight, neat and cool in front of Mr. Doowhee's desk.

Mr. Doowhee, replacing the two telephones attached to his ears with two others, and balancing another one under his chin, with only the receiving part to his mouth, motions for Randolph to have a seat, explains with a gesture of his left eyebrow that he'll be with him in a moment.

Randolph Alexander sits, brain impatient for the sort of airing he thinks it will receive in such high powered surroundings.

Mr. Doowhee (on the horns in his ears):

"Right! (left phone) ten mil and not a cent more! (right phone) So . . . I was just forced to tell her the truth, yeah! The truth! The more all she gave up, the less likely she'd be considered for the role, her ass being what it is. (left phone) Now wait! just one fuckin minute, my good friend! Whaddaya mean sixty-forty? I thought we were partners, even steven . . . seventy-thirty or nothing! (right phone) Tommy, ten mil and not a cent more, Oh . . . you accept? Fine! See if you can't get Marlon or Richard . . . with a ten mil budget I think we need a money-in-the-bank-face. Swell! Be talking to ya! Give my regards to the bitch, o.k.? Yeah! Fine! take care! (hangs up)

(right phone) "Well, o.k. so I says to her, I'll let you be

my mistress! The only thing I ask is that you gotta keep your body outta sight! I explained to her that I'd like to have her keep it completely outta sight. Preferably up at my summer place in Juneau.

"Yeah, sure ... She's up there now. Great piece of ass, Marty. Sure, why not? The key's under the doormat. Good deal, talk to ya when you get back, if you have any problems, call me, I'll straighten her out ... right! Talk to ya about that Slocum deal when you get back." (hangs up, the other phone rings immediately.)

Mr. Doowhee tosses off a hey-be-with-you-in-a-wink to Randolph. Randolph, trying to be Hollywood hip, shrugs suavely, not quite sure of what he's shrugging to, or on.

Mr. Doowhee (snide expression):

"Seventy-thirty sounds too steep to you? Listen to me, kiddo! Now you just listen! Ya tried to cut my throat with the Ketchum deal! Starved my kids outta new Bentleys with the Pepsco Deal! Your wife is keeping mine out of the Junior League with her malicious gossip ... and I'm absolutely sure it was you, you bastard, that sicced those Black Panther types on my oldest daughter. In addition to that, if that weren't enough, what about that little bit of blackmail you tried to pull on my mother's sister, her in the porno pix, with the goat and all?

"Seventy-thirty sounds fine, huh? O.k., now you're talking.

"Seventy-thirty it'll be. Take care, I'll be talking to you after my attorney draws up the papers.

"Oh, Charley? Did I tell you about the dinner party? That's right. 8:30 Friday. See you then."

Mr. Doowhee hangs up the last telephone, waves to Randolph in a familiar fashion, calls out to receptionist #1.

Mr. Doowhee:

"Shirley! No phone calls for the next ten minutes, I'm in a meeting. Right! Well ... o.k. If he calls, but no one else, got that?"

Mr. Doowhee switches off the intercom, turns to Randolph Alexander, Black Writer, with a carefully cultivated, warm, affectionate series of gestures, calculated to inspire good will.

Mr. Doowhee:

"Hello *there*, Randy, may I call you Randy? Good! Sorry to keep you waiting . . . but, as you can see . . . " (shrugs with the air of someone totally beaten down by business)

Randolph Alexander (trying to be Hollywood hip):

"Ohhh, that's o.k. I understand."

Mr. Doowhee (stepping from behind his desk, sizing up his prey):

"Randolph? Did you say I could call you Randy?"

Randolph (feeling confident now):

"Sure, why not? I'll call you Blahwee, cool?"

Mr. Doowhee:

"Fine! Fine! Fine! Randy . . . without further ado, let me say at this point we have a project here that you have been especially considered for. Your agent sent over ten chapters of your novel, 'The Bloody White Circles Niggers Get Caught In' and we loved it, every blessed page of it! There's something fantastic about the honesty, the integrity you used in dealing with the lives of the people in your book. I mean, Real Honesty! They lived! Breathed! Bled! I just loved it! We just loved it! Joe and I! Just a minute! Lemme call Joe in, he should be in on this!" (Mr. Doowhee rushes to the phone)

"Shirley! Get Joe for me, will ya, Doll?

"Hello, Joe? Listen, Randolph Alexander is in my office . . . no, the writer, not the waiter . . . hah hah . . . come on up. I'd like to have you in on this meeting . . . we're discussing the project. Good!" (hangs up the phone)

"Uhhh, Randy, would you like a cup of coffee?"

Randolph:

"No, no thank you . . . "

Joe Yessieur pops in.

Mr. Doowhee:

"Ahhh, Joe! Joe, this is Randolph Alexander, brilliant, unheard-of-as-yet-new-Black-Writer ... "

Joe fumbles through the Afro handshake, all quivering thumbs, trying to be liberal.

Mr. Doowhee:

"I was just telling Randy here how much we loved his novel, didn't we, Joe?"

Joe:

"Oh yes, yes, yes indeedy, B.D."

Mr. Doowhee (in a position of command on the edge of his desk):

"Randy, the assignment we have in mind for you is the sequel to 'Cotton Comes to Badass Mr. Shaft, Tick Rip Rick.' Oh, incidentally, what did you think of it? One of our biggest moneymakers, incidentally."

Randolph (deadpan, honestly):

"I hated it."

Mr. Doowhee (flabbergasted):

"Yeahhh, but Randy, you gotta admit a lotta people, a lot ... can I speak frankly to you?"

Joe Yessieur looks as though he had just had a catatonic seizure.

Randolph (graciously):

"Please ... "

Joe:

"Yes, yes, yes ... "

Mr. Doowhee:

"A lot of black people went to see 'Cotton,' judging from our blaxploitational reports, uhh, from our ethnic poll department."

Randolph:

"That's unfortunate. I think *we* showed poor judgment by going into any movie house showing such a piss poor representation of who we are and who we could be."

Joe:

"But ... but, why did they ... uhh ... you all go? if it was that bad, in your opinion?" (looks to his Boss for approval)

Mr. Doowhee (steaming):

"Yeah, why the hell did you ... they go?"

Randolph:

"The urge to relate, maybe. Don't forget, we went to see Step'n Fetchit and crap like that. I feel, in my opinion, that, even though *we* bring a very critical point of view to most *American* things, *we* kind of let our critical attitudes down some times, at the wrong times. Like towards 'Cotton,' for example."

Mr. Doowhee and Joe exchange smirks.

Mr. Doowhee (condescendingly):

"Well, that's your opinion, or course, and you're entitled to it, right Joe?"

Joe:

"Oh yes, yes, yes ... Of course, B.D."

Randolph:

"O.k., fine, let's git down then! I would come up with a sub-ject, maybe something that had something to say about one of *our* heroes or heroines, past or present."

Mr. Doowhee:

"Who've you got in mind ... Sidney? Diahann? Sammy? Harry? Lena?"

Randolph:

"They might be cool too, but I was thinking more of ... ooo ... maybe ... Nat, Sojourner, Mary McLeod, Angela, Malcolm, or maybe even Martin ... "

Joe (enthusiastically):

"Yes, yes, yes ... Nat Sojourner, helluva name for a lead character ... Angela Malcolm sounds really interesting,

123

really interesting."

Mr. Doowhee:

"Go on, Randy . . . sounds really interesting, really interesting."

Joe:

"Yes, yes, yes . . . B.D. Right on!"

Randolph (going into 3rd):

"Well now, dig it, it doesn't necessarily have to deal with either one of these figures . . . but it sure as hell would be a groove to have an intelligent, well thought out story about what the black man in America has, and is going through in America, rather than some more over-fantasized bullshit by some white screenwriter who has access to Exposure thinks we're going through."

Mr. Doowhee (bugged):

"Now just a minute, Randy! You know this studio is in the entertainment business, not the telegram business, if you want messages . . . "

Randolph:

"I understand, Blahwee . . . but isn't it possible to Say Something, to make a Comment on the State of Our Society realistically *and* entertainingly?"

Joe:

"Where'd you go to school, Randy?"

Randolph Alexander (proudly):

"I was born in school, Joe. The University of Hardass Knocks, Uptown Campus."

Joe:

"Uhh, yes, of course."

Mr. Doowhee (pissed):

"Go on, Randy . . . about the project?"

Randolph (off into it):

"Yeah, well, let's say, for example, we take the sequel to 'Cotton.' In the sequel, why not deal with some of the ideals, ideas, rhythms, motions, notions, and the culture of what makes a black man in America black?"

Mr. Doowhee:

"I can't really understand what you're getting at, Randy."

Randolph:

"It's very simple, Blahwee. Instead of making, or trying to make black movie stars caricatures of white movie stars ... why not make them movie stars within their own cultural frame of reference? or if nothing else, not inhibiting that.

"I mean, like, is it really necessary to have a black 'movie star' play James Bond, or John Wayne? in order for *us* to relate to him.

Mr. Doowhee:

"I'm still trying to understand, do we ... ?"

Randolph (gesturing wildly now):

"It's simple! So simple! When you think in terms of a sequel to 'Cotton,' think of a cat who deals, first of all, from within his frame of reference. And then, if you really have to have him deal with the rest of the Hollywood-TV-commercial-jive that has misled the American people into accepting the smell of, but not the true quality of pure bullshit, let him be the first to say it's bullshit 'cause if he doesn't know it, being black, no one does."

Mr. Blahwee Doowhee and Joe exchange startled looks. Randolph looks from one to the other, as though they were creatures from underneath an ice cold rock.

Mr. Doowhee:

"Randy, tell ya what, why don't you sit down and write out an outline, something you think might make a good sequel to 'Cotton.'

"Believe me, I think we'd be able to bring out some of your ... uhh, ahhemm, original ideas."

Randolph (cynically):

"Right on! Well, nice talking to you."

Mr. Doowhee (shaking him out of the door):

"Yes, nice talking to you too. Let's have that outline in by next week. I think we might be able to get together. Right, Joe?"

Joe (shaking hands, beaming):

"Yes, yes, yes ... definitely."

Randolph:

"Groovy! I'll have the outline in by Monday.

Randolph Alexander exits.

Mr. Doowhee (to Joe):

"There ya go, another bummer! None of these bastards wants to write a straight script, you know? A good piece of solid entertainment. They all want to be cute, do something *relevant*.

"Listen, Joe, contact I.W. Hack. Tell him I got a hot project in mind. I'd like for him to do the screenplay."

Joe:

"What about ... uhhh ... ?"

Mr. Doowhee:

"You crazy? You think I'd run the risk of going broke trying to say something, to make a comment on the goddamned racial problem?

"We're in the entertainment business, buddyboy! And don't you forget it. And we'll be in the entertainment business 'til some black producer comes along to compete with a bunch of *Relevant* Stuff. Dig it?"

Joe:

"Oh yes, yes, yes ... definitely, B.D."

4. Exterior—MCM—Day

Randolph Alexander walks slowly down the steps mumbling to himself.

Randolph:

"Dirty rotten motherfuckers! Dirty rotten ... "

5. Exterior—Blarney Brothers (hah!) Studio—Next Day

Randolph straightens the knot of his fashionable tie, reshuffles a briefcase full of credentials and starts onto the studio lot, rushing to keep his appointment with Mr. Flimflam Flammer, Producer.

Fade out.

Suicide For A Writer . . .

Walking all around the room looking for something, nothing seemed to be in focus. I walked over to the window and looked out and down . . . four floors, not too many, lots of people have lived after a twenty story drop . . . nawwwww, have to do better than that.

I sat down for a few minutes, feeling suddenly tired . . . ha! that's a laugh . . . getting ready to do myself in and I'm tired. Funny!

What the hell will tiredness mean after I'm dead? After I'm dead. What a complete, final thought that is.

Listen to that noise down there! Four floors up, above the street and you can still hear the damned crowd.

God, I'm thirsty! Wish I had a coke. Maybe I ought to . . . nawww, if I leave this room I'll be forced to live and I don't want any more of that, the damned people, the noise, the heat and cold, the struggle to Make It, traffic tickets, rejection slips . . . nawww, I better stay here.

Lemme see . . . Seven o'clock. now, I think I'll rest myself for awhile, and then I'll do it.

Damn! this bed is hard as a rock. A helluva view of the ceiling, look at that fly. Seems a shame that men waste so much of their time on the ground when there're so many ceilings to be walked on . . . ahhh shit! What the hell am I thinking about? Man can't defy gravity.

Gravity, now that's something to think about, laying here, that's what makes my head feel so heavy.

Damn my head hurts. Aww what the hell, why worry about something like that? What I ought to have my mind on is something pleasant.

Cecile, Cecile ... if only you could erase my headache. I wonder if I could bring the feeling we had when we first made love?

Nahhh, you can't do things like that. That's really funny. You can sleep with a woman for years and all you can remember about it is that it was good.

Sometimes you can go back to certain movements, certain expressions ...

Sweet Cecile, I wonder who has the word for her now? Old flames always seem to be ashes when you go back to 'em, even in memory.

I'm cold. Well, this is the fall of the year, why shouldn't it be cold?

Sure was cold up at Ford Ord in '82 ... five o'clock in the morning and there we were, standing at attention like a bunch of robots in a heavy fog.

Thick foggy mornings on the Monterey Peninsula, like the inside of a giant cough, til twelve or twelve fifteen, then the sun would burn through the fog ... burn it clean away, lay a taste of sun heat on you that felt incredibly good.

Never thought I'd find myself laying out on the damned ground, begging the sun to shine on me. Shine on me. Shine on me.

Tomorrow ... I won't be here tomorrow. I wonder who'll miss me? Momma probably will. Daddy? Nawwww, he'll look in the papers, see my name and probably turn to the sports page.

I wonder if Cecile will cry when she finds out about me, if she ever finds out. Was she a sentimental type?

Who else? Who else? My old schoolmates? Nawwww, they wouldn't have anything to cry about.

Wonder where they are now? The high school football heroes, the cheerleading beauty queens, the most popular student leaders, the hoity toity. I know where they are, driving buses, filing reports on the rising venereal disease rate, selling tickets to raffles? Overweight, dimple cheeked housewives? Who knows?

Maybe one of them is Somebody. Or Something.

I imagine a lot of them won't remember me. What does it matter?

I wonder if Death is really eternal? Wonder if I'll be reincarnated. I'd like to come back as a bull, always charging always charging.

Ahhhhh, what the hell! Why speculate about all this kind of shit? The proof of the pudding is in the eating. Hear that momma?

Lemme see, it's eight o'clock now. God! how time flies! What does it matter now? I'll be able to forget about time . . . that'll really be something . . . after all these years of punctuality: the clock, the time of day, the hour, the clock.

8:03. Never thought to notice how long it took to go from one thought to another. Now here I've been laying up on my ass thinking for an hour and three, four minutes, thinking . . . never had time to do that before.

Bet my boss will be surprised when he hears about me. Surprised for about two hot minutes. "Well, I'll be damned!" he'll say, and then he'll ask someone whether or not my desk was cleared of all my work before I . . . uhhh . . . "left."

Fifteen years, six raises, ten bonuses, a good rep and I'll be awarded a "Well, I'll be damned!"

Well, what could you expect from people who didn't know that you were really a writer?

Someone walking through the hallway? Couldn't be anyone looking for me, no one would have missed me by now.

Sharlene will think I'm working late. Damnit! I should've called her. Oh well, it doesn't matter now.

I wonder if my sons will understand? I think Steve will, he seemed to show a lot of insight when we talked about Hemingway's suicide.

Suicide ... what a weird sounding word. How should I think about it? Be great to think about it as a noble gesture, thumbing my nose at the world'n all that jazz.

Who was that Greek that decided to stop breathing? Can't remember his name. Shit! it doesn't matter. I'm copping out, no matter what my attitude is or my feelings are right now, it'll be suicide, self inflicted death to the world at large.

8:18. I'm getting hungry. Today is Friday and my Catholic wife will have fish, trout probably.

Too bad, I'll miss a good dinner tonight.

Wonder why I should think of all these things now?

I think I understand a little bit of something now, about how the Jews supposedly made jokes on their way to the ovens
.

How can you joke about Death? Very easily, I see. It's too real to take seriously, too real.

Wish I could break this watch. A hundred'n a quarter is a lot of bread to pay for a watch. Maybe someone'll have some use for it after I'm gone.

Wonder what they'll do with my body? I hate the idea of being buried under the ground ... wish they'd burn me up and scatter me out in the ocean.

That won't happen though, Sharlene'll use a hell of a lot of the insurance money to bury me properly. Shaw was right, people really are stupid about Death.

My damn stomach is growling like a lion. Sharlene probably is cooking trout too.

I'll do it at ten o'clock. At ten p.m. sharp; heyyy, how in

the hell will I do it? I just thought . . . I don't have anything to use.

That's a laugh. They run around screaming about safety first and I can't even think of a way to off myself.

Let me see . . . I could use my necktie for a hangman's noose. Nawwww, a broken neck would look too bad, I want to look like myself when I leave this world.

Who in the hell am I trying to fool? No need to try to fool anyone now. I'm here all alone and the piece is in my overcoat pocket.

Guess I can stop acting now, no need to pretend, don't have to come to grips with anything, anyone, anybody but myself.

Myself, myself, myself, my—self!

Wonder why I'm so tired?

Guess I should be, after laying up thinking about this step for the last two weeks, or has it been two years?

Wish I could write something or say something profound before I die. It would really be great if I'd gotten famous or something and I had picked these last few minutes to make all kinds of comments on different subjects, or something like that.

Wonder what Malcolm X would've had to say about things if he had been a suicide? Or Kennedy, Gandhi, Jesus, Mohammed, Confucious—or Chano Pozo.

Where did he come from? Chano Pozo, he doesn't belong in that group at all. I imagine Bird would belong, he sure would've had some things to say if he had lived.

"Bird Lives!" Who said that?

Ten minutes to nine and I can hardly keep my eyes open. I better check this pistol, be a shame to have the son of a bitch misfire.

Damn! this bed is hard.

38 Walther, Germany's best . . . this ought to tear the back out of . . . ahhhh, what does it matter?

131

Nine o'clock. There's that empty ceiling again. Maybe if I closed my eyes tight enough I could blot everything out.

Nawwww, doesn't work, closing your eyes doesn't do anything.

I used to really like to walk along the lake front late at night, looking at the lights out on the water; and it was spring for the twentieth time in my life and I had no one to share it with, what a helluva feeling. To be lonely.

Momma loved me but my father didn't give a damn. What had I done?

What a fabulous ass that African girl had, eighteen years old and mine for a pair of stockings and a couple packs of cigarettes.

North Africa! North Africa! Tunis! God! how I wanted to go back but then there was Sharlene, pregnant, Catholic, ashamed, talking about how bad Black men treated their women, forcing my hand.

Who else blows as well as Miles, down low?

The summer of '80 . . . Washington Park, baseball games, drinking bottles of beer, sweat running down . . .

Long, long discussions about what black people should be doing, or not doing, the whole damned country in a ferment, things happening, I was going to become the next Richard Wright, a hardon for every woman in sight . . . the next Richard Wright . . . hah!

Hair getting thinned out, wrinkles under my chin, high blood pressure. Wish I were nineteen years old again . . .

"But, baby . . . you know I wanted to go back overseas, that's all I've talked about since I got back."

"Well, you should've thought about that before you got me pregnant!"

"Can't you? . . . uhh, I mean, can't we? . . . uhhh, do, you know, something about?"

"Do something about what? I'm a Catholic, I was born'n

raised a Catholic, haven't we committed enough sin as it is?"

"Sharlene, don't get excited. Don't lose your temper, baby! What can we do?"

"We can get married. I've already bought a ring."

Sharlene, nine to five, the domestic life, intercourse without love once or twice a month, sometimes . . . rejection slips on the novel, the short stories, the television script.

"You're a good man, Marcus, I'm recommending you for the incentive award at the end of the month, that'll be fifty extra bucks in your jeans."

"Thanks a lot, Mr. Graham . . . I certainly do appreciate it."

"May I have your attention, please. The monthly incentive award of fifty dollars has been awarded to . . . Mr. Henry Nishigawa, of the administrative department."

Dirty rotten motherfucker! Always somebody else! Never me! Why? Why? Why?

"Ohhh, Marcus, listen, I didn't have a chance to tell you before now."

"Tell me what?"

"Well, I won't be able to go to the prom with you . . . something really personal came up and . . . well, I'm sorry but I won't be able to make it with you."

"Yeahhh, I understand. Thanks for giving me the good news four days from the prom."

"I'm sorry, Marcus."

"You wanna play end? Young fella, I admire your guts, but we already have three or possibly four of the best high school football players in the city playing that position."

"O.k. coach, how bout right or leftl halfback?"

"Tell ya what, son. Why don't you come out for the team next year. I mean, a lot of the guys will have graduated or quituated . . . hah!hah!hah! quit-u-ated. Git it? Anyway, you need about twenty more pounds 'round your ribs. Come on back'n give it another try next year."

"Thanks, coach."

"Hey! hey! knock! knock! knock! knock! wake up in dere! What're ya gonna do? Stay all year?! Ya only paid $10.50 . . . if ya wanna stay longer, ya gotta come up with more dough. Let's move it, buddyboy!"

"Huh? What? Who is it?"

"Me! the desk clerk! let's be moving! We got other people waitin for this deluxe room."

"Oh . . . thanks, I'll be out as soon as I'm dressed!"

"Rush it up, will ya?"

"O.k. I'm rushing! I'll be out in just a minute!"

"Goddamnit! It's 7:00 a.m. How in hell did I sleep this late? Oh my God! What will I tell Sharlene? I better get the hell out of here and get to work . . . think of something to tell her later. I'm hungry as a dog . . . need a shave too . . . "

"Hey buddyboy, let's be gettin' outta the room, huh?"

"O.k. . . . I'm coming, I'm coming!"

We regret that we are unable to use your story at this time, thank you for submitting it to Tick Tock publications.

Sincerely Yours,
Mr. Andrew Tick

BOOK TWO

Sunday, Sundays . . .

Chapter 1

The slurred hints of Albert Ayler, Hubert Laws, Berlioz, Rahsaan Roland Kirk, Virgil Phumphrey, alias Abshlom ben Schlomo, Jutta Hipp, Pharoah, Sun Ra, Toshiko, Miles, Coltrane, Duke and Bird above ⹁ . . cool spiralings of clear Kant, Aquinas, Tom, Dick, and Harry, Brother Hegel and Rabbi Spinoza; tainted smoke from singed, center cut chops, three day old chicken grease, Mongolian farts, barbecued fruit flies, fried snow balls and the tablas of Chatur Lal drifted, zig zagging, past closed doors, through murky passageways on the fourth floor, obscuring the pedestrian sounds of flushing toilets, grunting lovers, the strangled gurglings filtering up through the steel flecked clouds from the diseased streets.

Days and nights of endless blacks and whites, drum-thunder emotions, pigs pushing and punishing suspected suspects.

Everything is Everything.

In his second floor efficiency Fred King sprawled face up,

spraddle legged on the fake Persian blanket covering his sway-backed sofa, nursing a tight, cruel, persistent hangover, carefully studying the jagged cracks on the ceiling.

I ought to just lay here and let 'em burn. Damnit! If I do that I won't have anything to eat. Marvelous thing about rationality, it's always forcing us to do something we don't feel like doing.

Reluctantly, gracefully, he pulled himself into a sitting position, the veins at the temples of his narrow, dark, Hamitic face swelling with the effort.

He slumped, nodding slightly as the nausea settled itself into the pit of his stomach and with grave, shuffling steps, made his way to the two burner where a skillet with two burning pork chops sizzled.

Goddamnit! Burned anyway! Should've let them burn without any interference.

He turned the flame off under the sputtering skillet, stared at the charred chops with a cold expression on his face, and turned to urinate in the rusty little sink behind him. Oh well.

He labored back to the sofa, the veins throbbing in his temples. Settling in, his eyes searched for a new set of cracked patterns to stare at.

Sunday was always a bad day for Fred (who refused to believe that Monday had any importance at all) a completely discredited day, which he announced periodically, "has no rational reason for being."

Saturday yes, Sunday no. And most definitely not Monday.

Monday meant payment for all the time spent on the good times you had Saturday and ... aww shit! I'll just be late again tomorrow, they can fire me if they want to.

For long moments he lay stock still, coming alive to clasp his arms across his chest from time to time.

After a lot of thought about the move, he left his position to stroll over and stare out of the only window in the room.

A window on the side of the building, staring walleyed out onto the "El" tracks of 63rd Street, and the chimneys and swarms of black people patrolling the street below.

And back to his back on the sofa. A roach crisscrossing a jagged crack. The damned pork chops burned!

Why don't they fix that damned toilet? Shit!

I'll have to tell Samu to stop spraying into the cracks, he's chasing all the bugs into my room.

Fred! Fred! Knock, knock! Tellie-phone!

O Gawd! that's all I need to do now . . . talk on the phone.

Samu Akintola, the little Nigerian prince, stood in the hall grinning genially as Fred slugged his way out of his room, bumping into the door twice in the process.

"Fred, you con reely drink a grate deel. I saw you drink, at least, a fifth of whiskey last night. Thot was reely quite a party last night, huh?"

Fred edged past Samu chattering in the hallway.

Gawd! this little bastard loves to talk. He can't even call you to the phone without running his mouth off. The party was last night . . . guess he'll be talking about it for months. Ooohh, my head aches.

"Hello."

"Hiii Freddie!"

"Yes?"

"What're you dewing?"

Why must they always have to call me the next day and ask absurd questions. What're you dewing?

"Oh, nothing much. Laying on the sofa, staring at the ceiling."

"Meditating?"

"No, just looking at the ceiling."

"Oh wow! That really sounds groovy! Are you . . . are you alone?"

"Yep, just me and my crack in the ceiling." Why doesn't

the silly bitch come right out with it and ask if she can come over?

"Would you be interested in uhh having someone who. . .?"

"No, Joyce, not today. I have an incredible hangover and I don't feel the least bit sociable."

"Oh."

How I hate weak people sometimes, especially weak women!

"Oh, well uhh, I'll see you at work tomorrow then."

Probably. Work? Why the hell would she have to mention work?

"Bye bye Fred."

"Bye Joyce."

Fred placed the phone in its cradle and stood with his hand clenched around it, feeling disgusted. Why do American women have to diminutize every fucking thing? Even in this day and age. Bye bye, itsie bitsie, teenie weenie. Stop it, Fred, you're becoming bitchy witchy.

He walked slowly back to his room, past the clattering sound of Samu's voice, pulled the Brahms Second from his record rack and gently closed the door in Samu's face.

. . .

Darius X. Monzano. Mon-za-nooooo! Say it with some kind of feeling or else I'll mispronounce yours! Spooned a bit of scrambled egg into his dog's mouth, a handsome Collie with one grey and one blue eye, ruffled the mane of his silky, light summer coat with impulsive, nervous, indulgent pride and stared at the brown body of the girl laying over in the corner, on his dog's bedding.

Look at her, Sire. If it were possible to use her in the right way, you'd be a man, just like me.

The girl, at that moment, flung her arm carelessly over the edge of the pallet, felt the cool floor with the palm of

140

her hand and woke up to smile at the sight of Darius X. Monzano and Sire staring at her.

. . .

Mrs. Solomon lowered her newspaper and peered over the edge at the pale face in front of her, at the bluish tinge of a three day old beard.

Bet he only just shaved a few hours ago.

"So, what can I do for you, David?"

How proud he makes me feel to be a Jew. Look at him, so pale and thin, after all those horrible camps. And he always pays his rent on time. I wish some of the others would follow his good example.

"Mrs. Solomon, do you have a ladder I can use? The light in my ceiling is out."

Mrs. Solomon, moving quickly, despite her heaviness, reached into the keybox over her desk.

"David, for you I have a ladder. Come, it's in the basement."

. . .

Brahms' Second, jive bitches, smeared love affairs, collected studies of Peanuts, B.C. and Andy Capp, Miles, 'Trane, Ogun. Slipped discs and effervescent tongues, spinning canes twirled above the heads of candy striped women, Sunday morning in the towers. Awww shit!

"What are you doing, Leo? Writing another epic poem?" David asked.

"Maybe. Nawww, just scribbling some shit that's on my mind, that's all. Hey, where you goin with that ladder?"

"In my room the light is out, come . . . would you hold for me the ladder?"

Leo Hunter crumbled up a sheet of scribbled on paper, tossed it, set-shot style, into a corner wastebasket, closed his door and followed David Jordan up to the third floor.

"Hey man! You know somethin'? I really do dig the third floor, I don't smell the kind of shit up here that I smell down on my floor. You know what I mean?"

David, going cautiously to the top level of the ladder: "Yes, yes, there is a difference in smells, I think."

Leo, holding the ladder, sniffing around casually: "Whatchu got to eat, Dave? I'm hungry as a big dog!"

"Would you like some lox and sour cream? I have, also, some fresh bread."

"Ain't you got no ham? No bacon, pork sausage? You know, stuff like that?" he asked, with a quick broad smile up at the top of the ladder.

"Seriously speaking. Uhh, no, but we could go to the store for that, if that is what you'd like?"

David, the Beloved of God, in his slight gutteral way of speaking. Would give you the shirt off his back .

"Sho' would be a gas! with some grits and some momma-made biscuits. You hip to grits, Dave?"

"Uhh no, uh yes, I am hip" . . . calmly smiling . . . "to grits."

"Ahhh David, I see you found someone to hold the ladder for you. I suddenly remembered how shaky it was, so I came."

"Hi Miz Solomon." Downcast expression framed in the spaces between the rungs of the ladder.

"Hello Leo, where have you been for the last week? Every time I come to your door there is no one."

"Uhh, well, I been kinda busy, you know? Been studyin pretty hard."

"And how is the poetry coming?"

Large, world-gentled brown eyes staring out of crucified flesh, looking down on us again. Another great Jew gone to the Real Holy Land, singing internal songs so weird and melancholy that they inspire the need for any God we can get our hands on.

"Huh?"

"The poetry, how's it coming?"

"Oh, awright, I guess. Never seem to really be able to write what you think."

David, coming down carefully from the top of the ladder, mumbling. "One of the hazards of trying to create, I think."

"Yeahhh, guess you got a point there, bruh Lave."

"I leave you boys to your philosophies, I have work to do."

"I'll bring the ladder back down."

"Whenever. Leo, will I see you tomorrow?"

How subtle she is.

"Uh, yes Miz Solomon, sometime in the evenin, I'm expectin a check . . . "

She looked at him skeptically and shuffled off. And such a nize boy, too bad he won't ever amount to anything.

"You know something? that's really a groovy old girl. Ain't too many places you could stay in this city and get three months behind in your rent."

"Yes, that's true, not too many places in the world, Leo. Come, let's eat."

As David made sandwiches, Leo stooped to look at the books printed in German, something he always did whenever he was in David's room, trying to put something together about David being a German, his accent and being a Jew. It just seemed to be slightly contradictory, somehow.

"Lox and sour cream, huh? I think I've had this before, at somebody's house. I don't remember."

David, smiling slightly. Probably it was here. "How about some chess?"

"Why not? I haven't had a new hole ripped in my buns since the last time we played."

"What's that you say?"

"Uh, nothin, get out the pieces before I psyche myself out."

And if he isn't spraying bug juice around, or running his damned mouth, he's screwing.

Fred left his place on the sofa again, to turn the Brahms up a little louder, hoping to shut out the coarse, woolly sounds coming through the wall from Samu's apartment.

The low points, the gaps in the music allowed Samu's passionate moans, his involvement with his latest girlfriend, a Greek prostitute named Helena, to flood through.

An anxious knocking above Samu and Brahms.

"Yes?"

"Missus Solomon."

Fred, with a dry, neutral expression on his face, opened the door a pinch, peeked around the edge of it as though he were undressed. "Yes, Missus Solomon, what can I do for you?"

Fred, graciously smiling as usual. God, what an intelligent man.

They stood, making motions with their mouths, Fred suddenly aware of the loudness of the music, reached a long arm over to spin the dial down.

"Fred, believe me, as much as I love Mozart ... "

"Brahms, Missus Solomon, Brahms."

"Uh, yes, yes, of course, Brahms, as much as I love his music, when it's so loudly played it lacks something, don't you agree, Fred?"

Fred, lips pulled down at the corners, tightened crow tracks around the eyes. "Yes, of course, you're right."

He quietly closed the door, resisting the faint urge to tickle Mrs. Solomon's double chins, turned the record player off entirely and stood for a long moment, listening with intense concentration to Samu's rhythmic grunts. He smiled sarcastically. The little bastard just struck Brahms out, with the bases loaded too.

"Why do you call him Sire?"

"I call him Sire because he's full of fire and he's not for hire."

The brown skinned girl sat up, wrapping her forearms around her knees and laughed.

"Funny how people start lookin' like the animals they own, after awhile, like you'n Sire, for instance."

Darius, lighting a cherrywood pipe with a Lucifer faced bowl, winked into Sire's blue eye.

"Only natural that a man should look a little like his best friend, don't you think?"

"Well, I never heard it put that-a-way."

"However, it's interesting that you would see the resemblance between a man and a dog. Many women twice your age haven't been able to make that connection."

The girl smiled with firm, even white teeth.

"My momma is always tellin me that a man ain't nothin but a dog."

Darius, growling softly, clenched his pipe tightly in his teeth and crawled over to the girl.

"Maybe your momma got too much of it ass backward, when she was growing up."

The girl smiled sweetly, gracefully released her knees and laid on her back looking up at Darius.

"You're so young, Victoria, so awfully young. Where have you ever been in the world? Have you ever been to Heaven? for example."

"Huh?"

"Have you ever been to Heaven?"

"Wow! You shore do ask some funny ass questions at times!"

"Just answer me, luv . . . don't get intellectual about it."

Victoria cut her eyes into a corner, peeked around Darius'

face onto the ceiling. "Once, yeahhh, I been there once."

Darius' left eyebrow shot up into an inverted V.

"When?"

"Oh, 'bout a couple weeks ago. If we talkin 'bout the same place."

"Don't joke with me, young lady. You should know by now that I know the difference between the truth and a lie."

Victoria shrugged her shoulders, smiled ever so innocently, removed Darius' pipe with one hand, arched her back and with the other hand pushed the roundness of her pert young breast up to him.

Sire lay in place, watching his master suck the young girl's breast as she stared into the dog's two toned eyes with a strange, wild look on her face.

. . .

"I don't need to shoot drugs into my veins, or drink or become depraved or any of that shit! I am a whore on principle alone! I don't even need to be a whore for money! I am a whore because I have chosen to be one!" the Greek whore, Helena, said. With passion.

"What time is it?" she demanded.

Samu stretched out on the bed, sweat glistening on his small, taut, black body. He was proud of his body and that he spoke with hardly any accent. He often said that to many of his fellow Africans affected a strained, pseudo-British clip that made them sound ridiculous in America, especially in the black ghetto.

"It's 4:30. Why?"

"I must go, I have another date at 5:00."

Helena's sentence was punctuated by her swabbing between her legs with his dishcloth, crouched in front of the kitchen sink.

"Why don't you stay with me some more, you know I will

pay you?"

She carelessly tossed the cloth into the sink, walked over to the bedside, blondish pubic hair dense and curly with droplets of water in the half light of the curtained room.

"Do you think I would stay with you because you had money for me? huh?"

"I don't understand. You sell yourself for money. I have money. I will pay you more to stay with me."

"Stick your money up your ass, Samu!"

"I don't understand, I don't understand you a'tall."

Helena, pulling her slip over her bleached blonde hair, smiled coldly at Samu's throbbing penis twitching in mid-air.

. . .

"That's it, man! that's enough for me! three out of three is enough!"

David, smiling slowly through his grey teeth. "Well, perhaps if we change places, it would bring you luck?"

"Man, looka'here, ain't nothin gone bring me some luck but some coins, until I get that I'm gonna always be unlucked, dig it?"

And in the late afternoons, after the bagpipe skirlings and post hypnotic chess games, bagels, creamed cheese and lox (wouldn't Momma be surprised?) light brown skin Afro-American guy, New World 440 man, freebie feeler, dancing in place, pinched up by the nape of the neck, feeling for the pinhead of it all, frantically, trying to make sense out of no-sense, wanting to be the first Zen choirboy.

"Leo, don't you know of any girls, women you could, uh, uh, call up? We could, you know, have a party." Slight tinge of a British accent on top of the gutterals.

"Ain't that funny? I'm sittin here thinkin 'bout money and you got your mind on pussy."

Fred strolled in, nodding pleasantly, feeling for the first

time all day, the positive urge to be sociable.

"Heyyy, what's happenin, bruh Freddie? What pulled you out of your nest?"

Fred stared at Leo, trying to understand why Leo always called him "bruh Freddie," not just Fred like everyone else.

"Uhhh, how're things with you, Leo?"

"Just barely makin it, bruh Freddie, just barely makin it. Ain't too much else I can do."

"If you'd settle down into something steady and reasonable, pull your head completely out of your ass, it might be possible for you to be doing more than just barely makin it."

"O, dig bruh Freddie, I could hear the Brahms thang earlier this afternoon and it was a gas. Loud as you were playin it I guess half the neighborhood could hear it."

Fred and David exchanged skeptical glances, stared at Leo, trying to disguise their surprise.

"You . . . you like the second?"

"Well, naww, not really. Not quite as much as I dig Pharoah, Sun Ra, or Ornette Coleman."

"Leo, who are these people?"

Fred simply sank down onto the edge of David's bed, exhausted by the thought of the explanation he knew Leo was about to give.

"Awright, Dave, dig it! You have to be coming to these dudes from another place, I mean, you know, in order to really dig where they comin from, especially when they righteously git down."

"Is it still music? Why bother, there is no need to know Sun Ra. What a name! But wouldn't it be stupid not to know the Beethoven, the Bach or the Berg of this time?"

"Bruh Freddie, you must know somethin 'bout what to lay on bruh Dave here, he's lookin at me like I'm insane."

Fred shifted uncomfortably, took out a cigarette, lit it and began to lecture on the history of what has been commonly called in America ... *jaaassss*. He paused to light another cigarette after fifteen minutes of non-stop information had flowed from him.

"Goddamn! bruh Freddie! I didn't know you was into the whole thang! You sounded like Leonard Feather or somebody."

Leo bounced over to stand in front of Fred, to mop his palm, to lay skin on him, to reaffirm what he felt was the sort of funkiness that only black brothers knew about.

Fred, eyes half hooded, looked up to see Leo looming above him; his arm raised with the palm flattened to deliver the dreaded stroke.

Why do they have to do this? It's so meaningless, says nothing, creates nothing.

He dutifully held his palm out flat, properly, and Leo smacked it with relish, exclaiming and dipping a bit in the knees at the same time. Fred took the slapped stroke stoically. What else was there to do?

David looked from one to the other, liking both of them, intrigued by their individualities.

"Hey, dig y'all I gotta split. Got to go back downstairs 'n finish up some stuff. That motherfuckin Fred! Every time I think I've got my act together he comes along and blows me away again. If it ain't Hindu Thought, or ... or Inside the Other Side, it's something Else. Who would've ever thought that he knew anything about jazz? Listening to all that highbrow stuff.

"Come back up later if you like, Leo. Perhaps your luck will be better."

"Yeah, yeah, I just might be doin that, Dave. You want me to leave your door open a taste?"

"Yes, it's good, a little breeze would be welcome."

Leo bounced out of the room, a repetition of the rest of the rooms in the building, humming as he walked down the

149

hall.

Fred stood up, stretched, walked to the door and firmly closed it.

"Gawd! That guy really gets on my nerves sometimes."

"Leo? He's alright, Fred, just a bit young and undecided about who he wants to be. But how is that different from any of the rest of us, finally?"

Fred, ignoring David's question, took a couple hesitant steps up the ladder.

. . .

"Doesn't it give you a funny feelin to do it with a dog watchin?"

"Sire is not a dog."

"What is he then, if he ain't a dog?"

"He's a different kind of male."

"What do you mean . . . different. How different?"

"Would you like to find out?"

"Huh?"

"Would you like to find out how different he is?"

Victoria stared up into Darius' smooth red face, the inverted V hooks, his eyebrows, hanging question marks at her, and slowly nodded yes as though she were in a hypnotic state.

This dude is really cracked! This'll be the last time I run away from home and come to *this* crazy ass basement.

Darius rolled carefully off of Victoria's body, to her right side, impulsively pecking at her breasts as he did so, and turned to Sire.

"Sire . . . sssch!"

Sire's aquiline nose perked up at Darius' sound. He uncrossed his paws and ambled over to the pallet wagging his tail.

"You'll have to get on your hands and knees."

Victoria stared even harder at Darius, a light panic in her

eyes, looked quickly at the shiny red point of Sire's penis and rolled over on her stomach.

"Will he hurt me?"

"Do I hurt you? His paws might scratch your sides a little, but what is life without a little pain?"

Sire, sniffing and licking the juice from between Victoria's legs, mounted her as she knelt, holding the top of her head cradled in her hands. Darius pulled himself into a sitting position, calmly lit his pipe and smiled at Sire, panting and drooling saliva from his long pink tongue onto Victoria's back.

"Ouch! he scratched me, his paws!"

"He wants you to close your legs a bit, a little closer together. Yes, like that. That's it." Sire closed his eyes with pleasure as Darius scratched him gently, lovingly, behind the ears.

Chapter 2

"Awww, c'mon! C'mon, Helena! Tell me! How much did he give you?"

"What does it matter? All you ever think about is money. Money, money! All the time! Don't you ever think about anything else?!"

"Heyyy, looka'here momma! Don't be layin that kinda drama on me! If you didn't have anything but a couple cans of sardines, your rent was past overdue and you didn't know whether or not you were gonna be back in school next quarter because your grant had run out and everything else. If you didn't have any money or the prospect of gettin any . . . then, goddamnit! you'd be thinkin 'bout money! money! money! all the time too!"

She laughed roguishly at Leo's breathless speech and his contorted features.

"Aaah Leo, you are so funny. Sooo funny. Look, I will *loan* you twenty dollars. When will you pay me back?"

"Twenty dollars!? What the hell can I do with twenty dollars?"

Helena, with a sly smile, started to push the twenty dollar bill back down into her handwoven purse.

"O.k.! O.k.! O.k.! be cool!"

Leo bounced across his small room and, with thumb and forefinger, neatly plucked the bill out of her hand.

"Well, I *can* buy a lil wine and some more notebook paper and maybe go to see a good flick with this."

She took in his reasoning with a shrewd glance and smiled, a bit more compassionately. The true artist is always hungry.

"Is this what you're working on now?"

She pranced past him to look at the pages scattered about on his writing stand, an elevated drawing board with an old fashioned high stool tucked underneath.

"Yeah, yeah, I'm tryin to put some sho' nuf, fo' real avante garde shit together and it ain't comin out too swift."

She plopped down Leo's bed, scooched and positioned herself into place with some of his pages and started reading.

Leo wandered over to sit on the window sill, alternately looking down onto the street and peering up under Helena's dress as she sprawled on her back, shoes on, legs cocked up and apart.

"Mmmm ... some of this I like ... some of it."

"Awww, I betchu don't even know what you readin, you always say shit like, some of this I like, some of it."

She stretched her legs out and slowly lowered the sheaf of papers until they rested on her slightly bloated beer belly.

"I am a Greek, from Mikonos and we Greeks have forgotten, have lost more of an understanding for poetry, music, art and ... and ... I don't know what else! than the rest of the people in the world ever knew anything about!"

"Awright! awright! don't take me on your Greek-trip-thang

again! Please!" And he smiled warmly, to let her know he was enjoying her.

Helena returned his smile, disappointed that they were not going to indulge themselves in her favorite argument, and fumbled into her purse for a cigarette.

Leo left his place on the window sill, went into his closet, jammed with overcoats, Army shoes, books, odds with ends and pulled out a cellophane packet with three marijuana cigarettes inside.

"Here, smoke one of these, helluva lot better for you than those doll hair cigarettes you smoke all the time."

He pulled a nearby chair to the bedsie, propped his feet up on the bed and lit one of the joints. He passed it to her and took it back for a few silent hits.

"Tell me . . . suuuuck! tell me about Greece, baby."

"I cannot tell you about Greece, no one can tell you about Greece, you must go there. I can only tell you about Mikonos."

"Ain't that Greece?"

"To some people. If you had never lived anywhere else but Mikonos, then Mikonos would be Greece. For some people, Crete would be Greece, or Athens even."

"Well, awright then, cool! Tell me about Mykanos."

"Mikonos! Mikonos! I've told you a dozen times!" She sat up urgently and sprawled back, her eyes half closed, exhaling a small, round, clear stream of smoke.

"The first thing, the very first thing I can tell you about is the sun." She took another deep, expert pull on the marijuana cigarette.

"And, maybe, the bread I used to carry home from the bakery. Bread that was made in round loaves and had such a perfume about it . . . aaahhh! I can remember the smell with my eyes closed. Or, no! no! it would be the way the sea was in the afternoon. How blue it was and how green! the bluest blue and the greenest green!"

"Hah! you must be loaded, you sound like you loaded."

"But no, no, that's not what you want to know about Greece, about Mikonos. You want to know whether or not all the women were beautiful. Yes, they were, in different ways. Or who did what to who?"

"Uhh, not necessarily."

She passed him the joint and resettled herself again, seeming to burrow, animal like, into the most comfortable crevices of the bed, and lay there, scratching her crotch with sure, crabby strokes.

"Mikonos is a small place, you can walk around the whole island in two, maybe three days. I walked around, all over, criss-crossed it, went back and forth, in and out, for the whole eighteen years of the time that I lived there."

She suddenly turned her face into the pillow with frustration, angry at the thought of trying to use words to say what she felt. "On Mikonos, on my Greek island there was life! Feeling! A drama every day! And I don't mean any of this drummed up television junk that people use as an excuse for life here. We had Real Life! A baby being born or an old man dying, a birthday party where people celebrated the birth and not the day, a place where a man could be a man and not be concerned about what kind of a man he was, as long as he was a Man. People could think what they wanted.

"But, for me, above and beyond that, there was the sun. The sun in a way you could never know about it unless you were there and shared it with someone you loved."

She paused, rolled her head back over into the hollow of the pillow and moaned. "Aaaaaahhhh . . . to love someone . . . to love someone . . . to love . . . "

Leo held the stubby end of the joint out to her.

"Uh, can you hold this? Without burnin your fingers?"

She shook her head up from the pillow and nodded no.

"I don't want anymore of that, it doesn't do anything for me."

Leo nodded his version of understanding, took a final hit on the roach, rolled the leftover paper into a tiny ball and flicked it under the bed.

"Leo, have you ever been in love?"

He stared at her for a hard moment, stared out of the window, stared at the linoleum under the side of the bed.

"Well, have you?"

Leo, eyes reddened from marijuana, nodded sadly. "Nawww, not really. I thought I was, a couple, maybe three times."

"On Mikonos there was Love," she said in a solemn, weighted voice, "not the kind of love people talk about here, in these sterile ghettos you people call a country. There was Love, real love. The kind of love that drove men insane in the heat of the afternoon, drinking retsina and looking at the young girls . . . me! Love was me! Love was a developing woman, Leo! She was a goddess! love was me! Leo! She was . . ."

"I hear ya, baby! I heard that!"

"I was a goddess! worshipped! appreciated!"

"Them Greeks is really frantic dudes, huh!?"

"Noooo! noooo! no!"

She leaned up on her elbow, fiercely, making wordless gestures with her free hand.

"*I* was love on Mikonos, on a Greek island, in a place where Love was understood."

Leo squirmed around in his chair and recrossed his legs on the bedside.

"*I* was love. It seemed that I understood feelings there because I could, not because I had to. Can you understand a little of what I mean, Leo the Poet?"

He picked at the side of his nose and nodded, irritated with her insistency.

157

"My heart breaks whenever I think about how quiet it was, and how people looked into each other's faces as they talked about the heat, the sea, wine, sheep, goats, or how beautiful the fish was that they had eaten the day before, or how dumb the English were because they came to Mikonos and drank scotch and soda. You know what I'm saying, Leo? Even for me, a woman, on Mikonos there was wine, women and song."

Leo, looking puzzled. "I can dig where you comin from."

She stood up suddenly in the middle of the bed and, measuring the springiness of it, began to dance, first one way and then the other, judging her performance by the anxious look on Leo's face as he posed himself at bedside, ready to catch her if she fell.

After a few moves she crumbled into a heap, laughing. "That's the trouble with Americans! You always hold out your arms to prevent someone from falling, from injuring themselves. You don't hold out your arms to embrace, only to prevent someone from embracing!"

He shook his head as though to say no, no that's not true, but thought better of it, and simply stared at Helena, rolling around, laughing on the bed.

"Aaahh my friend! I could tell you about Mikonos! Yes, I could tell you about Mikonos if you were blind and had no eyes, if you were deaf and had no ears, if you were drunk and had never tasted ouzo. Yes, perhaps, perhaps I could begin to try to tell you."

"You really dug it, huh?"

She stopped laughing, stretched herself out on the bed and solemnly folded her hands across her belly.

"Yes, yes, I really dug it."

"Well then, if that's the case, why did you leave?"

"Why did I leave? Why did I leave?"

She paused, sucking her bottom lip meditatively.

"I had to go back to a place I had never been before and

158

the boat to the mainland only made one trip a day."

Leo nodded his head absently, in a way that indicated his lack of understanding of what she had said and began to search around his chair for the cellophane packet.

He found it, took another joint out, lit up, placed his feet back up on the side of the bed, sucking in and slowly exhaling as he watched Helena drift off to sleep.

. . .

Today is Sunday and as they say, all is well. My boys are doing what they usually do on Sundays.

I worry most, sometimes, about Fred. He seems so thin and angry. He listens to Mozart and drinks and thinks, I feel, too deeply about the problems of the world. I see him walking through the halls as though weights were being pressed down on his shoulders.

Such an intelligent, sensitive man, he must find it hard to be black. Too bad he isn't more like that little animal living next door to him.

The joys of Samu Akintola's life must be wine, women and song. Funny how different everyone is and yet how alike. Too bad some of us can't be more like others. If only Fred had some of Samu, or vice versa.

I wonder if Samu has been circumsized? Yecch! What a thought for an old widow.

Davidka, ah, Davidka . . . pure. That horrible tattoo on his arm. How lucky we were that Grandfather decided to relocate the family, before . . . before all of that happened.

No use I guess, to have nightmares for someone who has lived through them. If only I could have died just once for him if only something could have happened to let me know the pain he felt but none of that has happened. I remain a middle-aged Zionist not extremely religious with a four story United Nations type building and taxes to pay pretending that

I was once in a concentration camp.

Mrs. Solomon flushed the toilet, grimaced at the ugly plumbing-needs-work-sound of the mechanism and slowly walked through the first floor hallway to her office-home.

Should I put Leo out? His rent is three months behind, he seems like a poor risk and is destined to be nothing, unless he sells some of his poetry. And I doubt that that will ever happen.

But where would he go? What would he do if he weren't here, to have someone near enough to deal with his inadequacies.

A literary type you're becoming! Inadequacies! Leo. What an incredible name for him to have, my father's oldest brother's name and he was a poet, but not one member of the family ever gave him credit for being what he was. We should all be ashamed for the way we treat poets.

Perhaps I'm thinking of the wrong person to evict. Maybe it should be Darius and his dog. Darius, who takes young girls to his room, who starves himself half to death most of the time, feeding that crazy-eyed dog of his. Monzano is very strange, I think he might be a dybbuk.

. . .

"Well, how was it, Victoria . . . is Sire a good lover? What's wrong? Where're you going?"

"Outside! Away from here! I don't wanna be down here no more! Every time I come down here you get me all messed up with—"

"We are all messed up, Victoria, it's part of our heritage."

"There you go! Talkin all that intellectual crap again!"

She snatched her clothes from the floor near the pallet and, avoiding the look in Sire's glistening blue eye, rushed into the toilet. She stood with her back to the mirror above the washbasin, wrapped her arms around her body, to feel the

160

scratches from Sire's paws, her head twisted back to see better.

The tears came without any change of expression. I bet my momma would die if she ever . . .

The tears ran down the hollows in her face as she pulled her dress over her head.

"Ahah! there you are! we thought you had flushed your-self down the toilet."

Victoria rolled her eyes angrily at Darius and started toward the door.

"That's what I hate most about you, you always treat me like I'm dirt!"

Darius sneered at her.

"Sic 'er Sire! Sic 'er!"

The dog started a stalking movement, growling deeply.

He jumped on the door and scratched it with frustration as she escaped.

Victoria stood outside, holding the knob, breathing hard, frightened and angry.

"You dirty rotten creepy ass freak!"

Darius lit his pipe, fell back on the pallet laughing like a maniac, and called Sire to his side.

"Come, Sire . . . leave her alone. She'll be back. Don't worry, bitches always get in heat, it's part of their nature, but who would know that better than you?"

Sire sprawled out, resting his long snout across Darius' knees as Darius affectionately ruffled the fur around his neck.

. . .

"Day-vid? Day-vid?"

"Yes?"

"It's me, Victoria."

"Victoria, come in."

David opened the door wide, beaming.

"Where have you been? I thought you would be here yesterday. We have all missed you, haven't we, Fred?"

Fred gazed casually at Victoria and nodded, disdain for the sight of her wrinkled dress and bohemian sandals obvious in his expression.

"I don't think Fred likes me."

"Am I supposed to?"

"Aaahh, no, no bad vibrations, huh? I have some wine."

"Victoria, would you like some wine? Fred?"

"No, no thank you, David, I'll have to be going , see you."

After Fred's departure.

"What's the matter with him?"

"Nothing, really. He is just that way sometimes. Tell me, how have you been? What have you been doing lately? Oh, but first, the wine."

"Yeah, I could dig a lil wine. Whatchu got this ladder standin up here in the middle of the room for?"

"It . . . uh . . . it represents an easy way to get to heaven."

"Oh c'mon, mannn! You got to be jivin!"

Chapter 3

Sun, sea, an adjusted life, the magic of being on a charmed island full of space, freedom, light.

Nights cancelled by diamond flecked heavens, the music from millions of ten stringed guitars, ghosts of men in mustaches and dark caps, tangled in fishnets and retsina, the blue sea, the green sea, two seas, all in the same place, Mikonos.

Helena opened her eyes slightly and studied Leo's shoulders, hunched over his writing board, his pencil settling into a slanted position from time to time, as he paused to consider a new idea, or to erase an old one.

"Too bad you writers have to sponge on other people's experiences for things to write about."

"Huh? Oh, you scared the shit outta me! I thought some kinda supernatural voice had come in here. What did you say?"

She shook her head and made a wry face, not caring to

repeat herself. "What time is it?"

He looked at her as though she were the reversed picture in a microscope, her body seeming to come from a tiny speck into focus.

"Well, are you going to sit there staring at me, or are you going to tell me what time it is?"

"It's. Six-thirty." She must be the most punctual 'ho that ever lived.

Helen Papagallos, took me damned near a month to learn how to pronounce that damned name.

"Uuggh! I have a dry mouth, what do you have to drink, Leo?"

"Water?"

"Water? To drink? Water is to wash clothes and bodies, what do you have to *drink?*"

"I see where you comin room. We could do up this other joint if you want to get high."

"Noooo! Stems and leaves give me a headache. I need liquids to flush through me."

"Something to flush you out, huh?"

"Yes, exactly! Do you think leaves and stems create the urge to urinate?"

"Damn! Never quite thought about it that way. Guess you got a point there."

Helena sat up slowly, holding her jaws in the palms of her hands, looking depressed, the balls of her feet barely touching the floor.

Damn she's a lil bitty broad.

"Hey, don't look so down, I ain't got no wine but I know someone who has got some. That is, if you'd really dig some wine?"

"Yes! Yes! of course I would like some wine."

Leo hopped off of his high stool and grabbed Helena's hands.

"Well, come on then, let's git on!"

. . .

"Leo, you've come for more chess? Hello, Helena."

"Naw, naw, man, I'm here to drink some o' that Red Mountain you stuck off in the fridge."

"Oh yes, of course, help yourself. Do you know Victoria?"

The two women looked each other over, analytically, completely.

Leo, on the balls of his feet, bounced into the kitchen and poured himself a water glass of wine . . . speaking around the corner; "Naw, can't say that I do. Hi, Victoria. What's happenin?"

"Hi."

"You know, Helena, don't you?"

"I only just saw her once or twice," David answered.

"C'mon, man, everybody knows Helena."

"Maybe he is one of the few who has never had any reason to know me. How do you do, I am Helena Papagallos."

"This is Victoria Mace."

"Awright! awright! Now that we got all that shit squared away, let's drink!" Leo gulped his wine, poured himself another one and filled glasses for the others in the room.

"And here is to the Great Flush, he toasted, winking at Helena.

She looked vaguely embarrassed, but held her glass up coyly to honor the toast.

The afternoon grew loose, reminiscent.

"And believe it or not, to this very day, people won't go into that house 'cause they say haints is in there."

"Aw c'mon, Vickie! what do we look like to you?"

"No! no! no! It is true, Leo. Of these things I have heard a great deal. Poultergeists are something like . . . uhhh . . . haints. Be careful, don laugh at the supernatural," Helena

165

warned. "I knew a lady, a beautiful young woman who had lost her man to the sea, but . . . because of certain feelings, certain vibrations, certain forces, you could say, he was restored to her"

"Oh wow! How did that happen?"

Leo smirked, his eyes glazed from the wine. "That's what I like about young broads, they're so romantic minded they'll go for anything."

Victoria looked across the room, through the rungs of the ladder and threw the cap of the wine bottle at Leo's head. "Go 'head, Helen."

"Helena! is her name," Leo said.

"It is nothing now, when you look back to it, a simple story of a handsome young fisherman who was swept overboard in a calm sea. His fellow fishermen could never explain what had hapened. One minute, they said, Michael Dionysus Stavropolis was standing on board and the next minute he was gone, not a trace of him. They used their nets to search for him. They say, in the village, that he returned from the dead because his sweetheart's love was so great, so profound, her prayers so sincere. At any rate, a day after his disappearance, he was discovered walking along the beach with no memory of what had happened. He and his love were married and lived happily for many years, until he died. Again.

"My mother used to say that Melina Stavropolis had been widowed twice, once before marriage and once after."

Helena took a long sip from her wine glass. The room was quiet for a minute. Leo stared skeptically at the top of the ladder. Victoria's eyes misted over as she folded her hands primly in her lap and sucked on her bottom lip.

"Drink up Drink up! Everybody! Let us pretend it is someone's birthday or something, there is nothing to be gloomy about."

"Hey, that's a gas! Can y'all get ready for that? How 'bout

you, David? Let's pretend today is your birthday!"

Spontaneously, emotionally, Helena, Victoria and Leo gathered around David sitting on the bed, half lotus fashion, and began to sing.

"Happee birthdayy too youuuu . . . happee birthdayy too youuuu, happee birthday deeer Dayviid, happee birthdayyy too youuuu."

They burst into applause at the end of the song as David quietly wiped tears from his eyes.

"David, tell you what, I'm gonna go get this last joint I got and fire it up in your honor. Can you dig it?"

David nodded, still brushing tears out of his eyes.

Helena hopped off of the bed and staggered to the gallon jug of wine on the table.

"Births, deaths, everything should be celebrated with dancing. C'mon David! Victoria! Everybody! Let's dance!"

"But we have no music."

"Makes no difference! Makes no difference! None at all! We don't need music, we have our souls!"

Helena linked arms at the shoulder level with Victoria and David and slowly, in a graceful, stately manner, began to dance them around in a circle, circling the ladder, humming furiously pushing and pulling a bit at first, until they had interwoven with each other's rhythms.

"Hey y'all, dig who I found lurkin 'round in the hall!"

"Awwww mon, I wasn't lurking no place, I just heard some merriment and so . . . I thought . . . "

Helena quickly poured Samu a glass of wine. "It's good that you came to help us celebrate David's brithday."

Leo stared at the tribal slash marks on the little African hedonist's face, wishing that somehow they would redden, or in some way reveal what he felt about Helena being there.

Samu raised his glass to chest level and spilled a few drops on the floor.

"L'chaim!"

Helena clapped him on the back, causing him to swallow his chewing gum. "Soooo you speak Greek and now Hebrew too, huh?"

Their faces bubbling, swallowing glasses of wine, passing the lone marijuana cigarette around, and dancing with their arms linked, humming a hip little tune that sounded vaguely like the Volga Boatman.

Mrs. Solomon, passing by, framed the scene with her eyes.

"What gaiety! So much life!"

"Ooooh, Miz Solomon!"

The dancers stopped, glasses stopped trembling on the shaky furniture as they stared at the figure in the doorway.

"No! no! Don't stop for God's sake! So what's the occasion?"

"David's birthday!" Helena announced.

"Yeahhhh! David's birthday."

Mrs. Solomon rushed into the room, a frozen, painful expression on her face, and grabbed David by the nape of the neck, pouring kisses on his cheeks and forehead.

"David! David! You should've told me! You should've told me!"

The others looked curiously at Mrs. Solomon and David.

"Would you like a glass of wine, Mrs. Solomon?" Leo asked in a superpolite voice.

She abruptly unhanded David and turned to face the group, with a gracious smile for Victoria and Helena.

"Yes, yes, I would like a glass of wine to celebrate David's birthday. I'm sorry I don't know the two ladies?"

"May I introduce Victoria Mace?"

Victoria dipped her knees into the caricature of a curtsy.

"And the Greek lady from the island of Mikonos, Helena Papagallos."

Mrs. Solomon took a large sip from her water glass and

nodded grandly at the two younger women, offering her acceptance.

"So, don't stop your dancing for me. Go on! Go on!"

Mrs. Solomon sat heavily on the bedside and watched as Helena led the small group back into a circle around the ladder.

The afternoon shadowed itself, tipsy from two more bottles of Red Mountain and conversations that ricocheted and split at the seams, sometimes.

. . .

"Remember when marijuana was illegal? All they asked us to do was not get caught, that's all."

"Don't you understand, Leo? That's not the point, as to whether something is legal or not. I'm speaking of the unethical situations."

"Awww shit! You talk about ethics! A whole bunch of things in this society are unethical but they still legal."

"Ahhhh yes, Leo . . . but of course . . . "

. . .

"Have you known Samu very long?"

Helena slanted a sly eye in Victoria's direction, a quiet moment for "girl talk."

"Long enough. You want some more wine?"

"Yes, as long as there is some. Victoria?"

"Huh?"

"I have a question for you."

"What's that?"

"Why are you here? Sleeping around from room to room."

"I've even heard that you sometimes sleep with that evil man in the basement."

"Hey, now just one minute, Helen!"

"He-lena!"

169

"Helena, just a minute. Number one, I guess, is that I like being here, I dig being around groovy people. And anyway, that's a helluva question for you to be coming down on somebody with! You, of all people!"

"Please, no moral outrages please. I've had all I could stand. It was just an honest question."

"End of girl talk."

. . .

"So, sometimes on the High Holidays, a spirit, a feeling so rich and full would come to us, would make everything on those days seem so special that we children could hardly wait to hear the questions asked and the answers given. Was it that way in your family, David?"

"No, no, it was very different with us. Our famly was not especially religious, not unitl the Night of Glass ... "

. . .

Miles Ahead, God in His Heaven, the Devil in His Hell, all the rest of us in between, our ears snatched up by the noise of faulty plumbing, our noses opened to and by unusual smells and feelings.

Never on Sunday. Sunday is a good day for Crucifixion, for dreams, a stick of good herb, a willing cunt, art, music, good times, life, Samu drumming Helena's head on the bed. She, wonderful good natured 'ho, brings me—*loans* me the money. God, why can't I pimp?

Nabakov, chess the Bible Torah Talmud Upanishads Veda Shanti Shanti Shanti Koran (As Salaam alaikum lost and found brothers) Qu'ran, contracts with a Contact to do Some Something about us to us all of us to prevent us from being cheated out of a piece of the Action.

Oiche Chernya, or something like that, or could be if the Devil kept his paws off of her long enough and there was a way to make friends with that grouchy bastard upstairs.

Maybe the Way is chess hurt tattoos brown gentle eyes soft gutterals and love but what would happen if you had to marry one of them?

Uh huh, that's right another extension another dimension another declension. Lord, why was I sentenced to do my time in this dull ass place with all of these plastic/spastic valves?

Facts. Money speaks business is business and why didn't they leave me alone when I was in Afrika? Samu with his cheeks slashed wonder what those slashes mean? Too bad I don't have something like that on my cheeks.

Head is beginning to spin a little, I think I should be going. "So much wine I haven't drank since my Aunt Sarah got remarried. David, for you I'll say prayers and happy birthday again."

"Thank you, Mrs. Solomon, good night."

"You think she really thought it was your birthday?"

"Why not? We all need to celebrate something, sometime."

Chapter 4

Brahms, Satchmo, the Family of Man, D'artagnan, sirens screaming, prisoners asking to be unprisoned, in prison, Samu cold coking in the Greek cunt, trying to reach Him on a shaky ladder, swollen ideals milked from shabby deals, chops with the claps Mingus and Monk almost zapped by the shit, hot snow in a frozen nose, virgins in perpetual heat, sour nuts hanging between dreary southern thighs, sweet'n sour blacks, splashed up in the latest . . . why don't Jehovah's Witnesses stay home on Saturday mornings, what's the deal with them anyway?

Kim Novak used to, well, that was after she moved to Hullywood, anybody can be expected to do anything in Hullywood. Too bad she couldn't really act, but she had a nice set of nipples and buns.

That's what Dreams are made of.

Fred reached over the arm of his fold-out sofabed to the

173

stool parked beside it, clenched the exploding alarm clock in his fist, his middle finger frantically searching for the alarm button. With his eyes, still closed, he found the button and pushed in with all the pressure he could manage.

The echo of the clanging from the clock sounded through the room, and through Fred's skull. Monday.

He rolled away from the clock's mocking face, curled himself into a fetal position and buried his head in his pillow.

Monday morning.

He lay there, not fully awake, not completely asleep, hating the idea of being forced to leave his place in bed to try and create the whole thing again. Every Monday.

Why keep trying? It hadn't worked out too well so far, why keep trying?

Monday, and the realization of all he'd ever said about it slid back and forth in his mind as he stretched himself out and began to casually pluck at his pubic hair.

Oh well, what the hell, I guess I may as well get up, I'll be late anyway.

He slid slowly from underneath his covers, noting, in a sensitive moment, the change in temperature on his naked body as he lit his first cigarette of the day and hawked up last night's phlegm.

The Monday morning ritual had started. Urination in the sink, a silently asked "Who am I?" in the mirror above the sink, coffee pot on the burner, a slow, calm shave with Noxzema, piddling around for a pair of black socks and the right slacks, another cigarette, Ravel on the FM, the busting open of a Chinese laundry box to find the shirt that was already hanging in the closet.

Sports shirt? No, too sporty, hate short sleeves anyway.

He finally pulled a long sleeved, royal blue turtleneck over his head, stumbled into a pair of red and black slacks, cinched his waist with a handwoven belt of Mongolian horse hair, and stood looking critically at his image in the mirror, congratulating himself on the coordination of his garments. After a long moment, with an impatient gesture, he undressed, moving from royal blue, red and black to burnt orange and blue velvet.

In between changes of clothing, he brushed his teeth ... twice, took the perking coffee pot off of the stove, decided to have tea instead, and hummed the last movement of the Beethoven 9th as he changed back to his original outfit.

He stared out of his window, trying to remember the name of the cloud formation coasting by, and down onto the streets where people rushed along, trying to make a streetcar, bus, El, or something that would take them to where they thought they wanted to go.

He took one final sip of tea, gave himself one last, disapproving glance in the mirror and stiffly strolled out of his room.

Samu, coming out of the toilet across the hall with a towel wrapped around his waist and a newspaper under his arm, almost bumped into Fred.

"Aaaah, Fred, you're on your way to work, eh?"

He, tall and solemn, looked down onto the top of Samu's head.

"Yes, yes, Samu, I am on my way to work. How did you guess?"

"Oh, I can tell, you know?"

Why doesn't this little imp have some sense of ... of ... of ... something? Subtlety, maybe? He is so ... so what?

"Goodbye, Samu."

"Hah hah hah, o.k.! See you later, Fred."

. . .

"Ooooh no ... "

"Hi Freddie!"

175

God, why are the most banal people addicted to diminutives?"

"Good morning, Joyce." Watch her ask me a banal question.

"What did you do yesterday, Freddie? After we talked, that is."

He stared through the Mickey Mouse rims of her glasses, into her watery blue eyes and at her red tongue as it flicked from one side of her bovine mouth to the other.

"Well?"

"Nothing, nothing much. I just, uh . . . "

"Morning Mr. King!"

"Good morning, Mr. Goodrich." If that son of a bitch hates me as much as I think he does, why doesn't he stop being so damned polite.

"You were saying?"

"I just went back to doing what I was doing."

Joyce, coyly: "And what, may I ask, were you dewing?"

Why can't I think of interesting, witty, sophisticated, complicated, intelligent things to say to him? Every time we talk, every time he grants me a few minutes to run my mouth I feel like an idiot, a twenty seven year old idiot!

I knew she would ask that.

"Why don't I tell you all about it later? I have tons of work on my desk."

"Lunch, how about lunch together?" Stop! stop being so frantic for him! have some pride!

"I don't know if I'll be able to take lunch, I have a lot to do. Why don't I give you a ring before twelve?"

"That'll be fine, I'll be expecting your call, see ya later."

"Yes."

That stupid bastard Goodrich! Fawning around . . . you'd think it would dawn on him, somehow, that he doesn't know his ass from a hole in the ground. And Brookins! How incompetent can you get?

Look at all of them! Creeps!

"Howsit going, King? Gettin much these days?"

"Morning, Norris, how are you this morning?"

"Oh, pretty good for an old coot, I guess. It's you young whippersnappers with the tiger by the tail now."

"Yes, I guess one could put it that way."

Fred sat at his cluttered, battleship grey colored, metal desk, in the east wing of the museum clerical services department, cutting out tiny, flawed paper dolls. And looking, casually from time to time, at the integrated faces of the people around him, America.

The sham of it got on his nerves sometimes. The white guys who wanted to forget their history and buy him a drink, the black guys who were too conscious of their history to enjoy drinking with, and the yellow guys who gave the impression of someone dancing to a different music with each foot.

They pretended that they had too much in common, even the women, except for Joyce Markissian, who loved him because he was black and, for her, beautiful, exotic and Different. She was an honest person.

"Whaddaya say, Fred, how's about pullin somethin offa the old garbage wagon?"

"Doing what?"

"It's ten o'clock, break time. Aren't you having somethin?"

"No, I think not, it'll spoil my lunch."

"Okey dokey, suit yourself, guy."

You're fucking right I'll suit myself, you clod! They ring the damned bell and the spit swells up in the side of your head. They've been ringing your damned bell since you were born, I can just see your mother now, with her nightie night milking cap on, tinkling a bell against your ear and shoving a nipple in your face.

Awww shit! I guess I ought to go get a cuppa coffee, it might help me keep my eyes open.

. . .

"Freddie? this is Joyce, are you going out to lunch?"

"I hadn't really thought about it."

"But . . . don't you remember our lunch date?"

"Lunch date?"

"This morning, remember?"

"Oh yeah, this morning. I remember."

"Meet you out on the front steps in five clicks."

"Joyce! Joyce?"

"Yes?"

"Is it really necessary to drive so fast?"

"Oh, am I driving fast? I wasn't aware. The hour goes so fast you just sorta want to stretch it out as much as possible."

"I understand that, but there is also life before lunch to be considered, and afterwards, if the lunch was worth eating."

"Table for two, sir?"

"Yes, I called for a reservation. Joyce Markissian and friend."

Fred established a reserved, clammy expression on his face.

Why Gordons? almost everybody and everything I hate eats at Gordons.

The maitre d' pranced in front of them, a small load of menus under his arm, flicking his fingers at the busboys and counting the lunch hour crowd over and over under his breath.

"Here you are, Madame, sir, a waiter will be with you shortly."

The maitre d' pulled a corner table out to ease Joyce's ample hips into the seat, put an oversized menu into their hands, patted his marcelled toupee and pranced back to the entrance.

Gordons, she would want to come here, to this fake, pretentious, New-Old World crap!

178

As Joyce studied her menu from top to bottom, fluffing her almost blonde hair away from the sides of her face from time to time, he lowered his menu to study the people and the place.

The loving-lunch-hour-couple caught his eye. The woman tilting her contrived look of admiration up for a macho peck on the nose.

Bet if you threw both of them in bed right now, minus an audience, they wouldn't know what to do with each other.

"Oooo Freedie, don't you just love this place? The atmosphere 'n all?"

Fred, startled, looked around the corner of his menu into Joyce's beaming, flushed face and nodded yes, quickly.

"What're we having?"

"Let's have some wine, first"

Joyce scooted closer and gently placed her hand, all warm and moist, on Fred's knuckles.

"Don't worry about the check," she whispered, "I have some money."

"I'm not worried, Joyce. I'm not worried about anything."

"Oh, I didn't mean that exactly, it just seems that you're so far away, so distant sometimes."

The waiter, a slim, snake-eyed type with a distinguished scar in the corner of his mouth, poured a few drops of red wine into Fred's glass, straightened up, ignoring Fred's disgusted reaction to the sourness of the wine, nodded to another table signalling for their check and turned back to Fred and Joyce, filling their glasses as though the only consideration they could make was acceptance.

No wonder she's overweight, eating like that. It's a wonder she doesn't weigh a ton.

"Ummmmmm, good, isn't it?"

If I could stop it from walking around on my plate it might be good.

"Hah! Hah! Hah! Oh Freddie, you say the funniest things sometimes . . . Is it really that rare?"

"All it needs is a red cape to do its number with."

"Why don't you have them cook it some more?"

"Wouldn't make any difference. If I sent it back, they'd probably overcook it. A lousy bunch of culinary conspirators out there in the kitchen waiting to take over, after they've fed us all the lumpy potatoes, sour wine, salads drowned in salad dressing, three day old bread and stale butter we can eat."

Joyce slow motioned her actions, a hunk of juicy meat poised between her plate and mouth, and stared at Fred's profile. Her eyes swept carefully from his profile to the half empty bottle of wine, and back. She smiled at him, the steak puffing out the side of her face.

Service by gangsters, a plain, ordinary dump with white tablecloths, poor lighting and sour wine and they call this an "In" spot!

"Will that be all, sir?"

"Do you think we could stand anymore?"

"Beg pardon, sir?"

"Skip it."

"Fredie, let's have some more wine, or a cognac. Yes, how about a cognac?"

"Oh God . . . "

"Yes, yes, why not? Two cognacs, please."

"Yes sir, right away, sir."

"Don't you think you'll ever be able to love anyone, Freddie?"

"That isn't the issue, Joyce. That is absolutely not the issue at all. I see being able to love someone as a matter of will, not a predetermined event on the agenda."

I hate him at times . . . his arrogance . . . his fucking intellect . . . his way with words, his indifference! She slouched against the back of the booth, slowly twirling the cognac in the palm of her hand, the way she'd seen it done in the movies.

"It's all related, somehow. Love, art, music, defecation, immigration, how often you blink your eyes, what kind of tea or whiskey you like, what your mother's maiden name was, or whether she had one, which college or which grammar school you did or didn't go to ... "

"Freddie, I don't understand, what're you talking about?"

"I don't know, let's drink up and get out of here, I still have loads of work to do."

"We're going to be late."

"Doesn't matter, I'm always late on Monday anyway."

Joyce, nervously brushing her hair back with fluttering hands. She actually looks pretty at times, really pretty. Or is it the wine and cognac?

"Freddie, I think—may I speak frankly?"

"Of course, if you don't keep us sitting out here all afternoon. It's now 1:15."

"No, no, it won't take that long."

Fred stared into the sky above Joyce's head. Funny how different one's perspective is from an open car, a convertible.

"It's never made any difference to me, what people said, or how they've looked at us or what they think or any of that. I just know how I feel about you and how I think you feel about me."

"Huh?"

"What I'm trying to say is, this, Freddie. We may be able to fool the world but we can't fool ourselves."

At the conclusion of her statement she dropped her head onto his chest with the weight of a cannon ball.

He sat, cradling her head to his chest, brushing the hair back from the side of her face, looking up into the sky.

"Joyce? Joyce?" he called gently into her ear, "come on, let's go in now ... we're late."

She quietly pushed herself off of his chest and sat up straight behind the wheel, a trickle of tears running down the sides of her nose.

"Fred, does it make any difference that you're black and I'm white? I mean, does it make any difference in our relationship?"

He brushed face powder stains from his shirt front, got out of the car, walked unsteadily around to the driver's side and helped her out.

"Does it, Freddie, does it?"

"Yes, of course, it does. If it didn't you wouldn't even have it on your mind."

. . .

Darius X. Monzano nodded pleasantly to Fred as they checked their mailboxes. Fred took no notice of Darius, or of Sire, whose tail stopped wagging as he passed by.

"Ahah, Fred, how was it today, mon? Did you work your fingers to the bone?"

"No, Samu, as you can see, I did not."

"Hah hah hah, Fred! You are too much! Too much! Too much! You know I was just thinking today about that time we had at the picnic, remember last year when . . . "

Fred touched Samu gently on the arm to close his mouth, pointed dramatically at his head and rolled his eyes to indicate he had a headache, quickly unlocked his door and went inside. He flopped across his sofa bed, dangling his wrists over the side, seeking relief.

"Fred! Fred! tele-fone! Knock! Knock!"

"Jesus H. Christ!"

He pushed himself quickly from the bed, opened the door, cut a severe frown at Samu and picked up the dangling receiver of the hall phone.

"Hello, Freddie?"

Yes, Joyce . . . come on over. Make it about eight . . . that'll give me time to shower and . . .

"I . . . uh, was going to suggest that . . . uh . . . that you come over here. There's a really good movie on television tonight and, knowing that you don't have a television, I thought I'd invite you over."

"Thank you, Joyce . . . I'll see you about eight."

"The movie comes on at six-thirty, you know, the early show?"

. . .

The Great Pimp's workshop, Earth. Starved days and reckless ways.

Streets, names with day signs, Monday . . . a dead end. Yesterday impatiently waiting for a recycling.

American made, America north, a dedication to the clock's crucifixion, men and women assembled to do what they're programmed to do, by all the programs.

Girls who will never be women because bad imitations were their ancestors.

Boys promoted past tears, feelings and other essentially human qualities.

Blacks and whites, always trying to love each, in spite of the common past. Makes a lot of sense, doesn't it?

Chapter 5

Sorry, Sire. Scrambled eggs again. No meat. The smell of cat in your nose and you'd probably rather smell Pekinese piss any day. Yugoslavian shorthairs hairless Chihuahuas, Irish redheads, black wireless terriers, Circassian longhairs, pooty-bred Poodles, German bitches, Russians with airs, Afghans, Chinese snots, all of them in heat ...

He gracefully hunkered down on the neatly arranged pile of blankets, jerked his head up at the sound of an indistinct noise from beyond their door, identified it as the sound of someone stumbling up the first floor stairs and slowly, as the noise faded, crossed his paws and rested his snout on top of them, regally.

The well modulated tones of a pseudo BBC-FM announcer made his ears twitch as he nodded off ...

"And you definitely feel, Sir Anthony, that there will be no prospect of peace in the few-ture ... not even, say, in the next twenty years?"

"No, of course not! The Mexicans have a saying, quite intelligent people, the Mexicans ... "

"Yes, yes, right so, Sir Anthony."

"The Mexicans have a saying, they say, every now and then peace breaks out. I don't recall the words in Spanish ... unfortunately, we are not Mexicans."

"Uhh, thank you very, very much. Ladies 'n gent'men, we have been listening to Sir Anthony Armcrook-Crankshaw, Nobel prize winner, world famous mathematics teacher and raconteur, discussing our topic for the evening ... Prospects for Peace in Our Time. This has been, yours truly, Devonshire H. Montague, station U.S.S.A., 10.6 on your FM dial, inviting you to join us again this same time next month."

Darius flicked the dial around rapidly, twisting it past Bolero, the Quartet in F Major, through a slice of Shubert's Trout and into a piece of Shostakovich's Violin Concerto and finally, off.

Darius turned to look, sadly, into Sire's blue eye, gleaming out at him like a piece of glazed ice and shrugged. Sire closed his eyes and flopped over onto his left side.

Must be tough on you, Sire ... this heat. Bad enough for us hairless apes in the summer, I can imagine what it must be like for you.

Sixty First and Dorchester, Chicago, Illinois.

Sire twitched in his half sleep, his body shaking from the spasm. Darius leaned against a corner wall, tamping his pipe underneath a print by Chehi Babbo, listening to the Monday night sounds.

Dumb bastards! Shuffling in from their illusions, stopping off to narcotize themselves with Sartre, Sukarno, newspapers stashed under their flushed out armpits. When will they realize it's all down here, isn't it, Sire?

Sire raised his head slightly, feeding on his master's comments, and with slow, sure movements, arranged himself in a better position to scratch behind his left ear. Darius watched the scratching intently, his unlit pipe dangling from his mouth like an unanswered question mark.

Sire finished his scratching, flopped back down on his right side and closed his blue eye, the grey one gleaming at Darius.

Darius leaned away from the wall, fascinated by the eye and wondering, as usual, whether or not Sire was asleep.

A bold, triple stroked knock jolted both of them. Sire's back stiffened and his blue eye popped open as he worried his nose around into the upper scent levels . . . danger.

Darius withdrew his pipe and asked in a seductive voice, "Who is it?"

Sire slid his tongue out slightly in anticipation.

"Helena," a voice answered.

"Helena who?" Darius asked, a cold smile sprawling across his mouth.

"Helena Papagallos! You son of a bitch! Who did you think it would be?"

Darius looked quizzically at Sire, holding his pipe at half mast.

Sire beckoned impatiently with his nose . . . let the bitch in . . . let the bitch in . . . grrrrrrrrrrrr . . .

. . .

"In the beginning, even, it was bad but not quite as bad as it became later."

Victoria turned onto her side, cushioned her head in her hand and tried to look into David's eyes in the dark. "How old was you?"

"How old was I?"

"You know, when they started puttin y'all in them camps 'n stuff?"

What could I tell her, make it possible to understand the

187

anger and fear and lack of feelings altogether, the insanity of one day being normal; of being warm, safe, clean, loved, praised, well fed, and then of having it all pulled away and exposed naked.

Death and people dying freezing to death, burned to death, poisoned, shot, gassed, starved, beaten ... death, the final solution.

"David? David, you 'sleep?"

"No, no, I'm not asleep. The year was 1939 and I was twelve years old when they came for us. I was bar mitzvahed in Dachau."

"You was what, where?"

She is so beautifully ignorant. No awareness, no sense of the ugliest memory ever to have occurred on earth.

Victoria playfully tickled David in the ribs.

"C'mon, old man! You gon talk to me or go to sleep or what?"

He smiled uneasily in the dark of the room, knowing that the last thing he'd be able to do was sleep.

"I am going to talk to you."

"Well, c'mon then, talk! I asked you a question. I asked you two questions! We been rappin steady for 'bout the last fifteen minutes and seems like every time you start off goin somewhere you wind up goin to sleep."

"Aaaaahhhh, no, no, Victoria, not asleep. I am just pulled back by memories. Do you have any more cigarettes?"

"Uh huh. I didn't know you smoked, David."

"Yes, sometimes."

Victoria reached down to the floor beside the bed, shook a couple cigarettes out of the pack, lit both and passed one to him. They relaxed side by side, cigarette tips glowing in the darkness, noises coming from the streets.

"A bar mitzvah is when a boy comes of age ... "

"Like a birthday?"

"Something like that, except for it being much more important, in many ways. Dachau was a concentration camp, Buchenwald was a concentration camp, Auschwitz was a concentration camp. I spent six years of my life in the camps. I was twelve years old when, as I once heard a man say, some Germans became Jews and other Germans became the Gestapo.

"I was twelve years old and I was just like all the other children, I felt. I did not think it was strange that my parents would not allow me to go out to play, or that I was not allowed to do this or that. I was an obedient child and children did not question their parents in those days."

"Did you have any sisters 'n brothers to play with?"

My sister Sarah with a bayonet in her rectum Sarah stumbling through the streets with blood running down her legs. My mother ashamed for the neighbors to see blood running from underneath my sister's dress fifteen years old a virgin.

Rachel on the floor her clothes torn off a knee on her throat a boot on one wrist a boot on the other wrist her legs pulled apart. My father, his jaw broken, his arm broken, Jakob thrown out of the window. My mother already dead of shame before the camp. My father, my father dying more slowly.

"Yes, yes, I had two sisters and a brother to play with, my oldest sister taught me to play chess, my older sister, Sarah."

He crushed his cigarette against the wall, grinding it slowly as a small shower of sparks fell to the floor behind the bed and died, one by one.

Victoria watched the scattered sparks, shocked to see David smear ashes on the wall. They lay very still, Victoria smoking and waiting, not teasing him about being asleep or awake.

"They marched us for miles, through the streets of the city, along with the other Jewish people of the city. Before we were at the cattle cars there were only three members of my family left."

"David? I thought you said, I thought you said that you had a brother 'n two sisters ... "

"They were wounded and could not continue ... so ... "

Victoria wrinkled her brow into a tight frown and slowly crushed the butt on the floor.

"You wanna 'nother cigarette?"

"Yes ... "

Sarah, holding her insides falling out being stomped to death by men with machine guns. My father, jabbed in the eye with the barrel of a rifle; my father always strong pushing his eye back into its socket; my mother, her shame forgotten, my mother trying to help him. How can they say they did not know what was happening?

He took a deep pull on the cigarette and watched the dim spiral of smoke as he exhaled.

We were whipped into the cattle cars and left there ... hundreds of us jammed into each car ... for three days and nights.

Why is it possible for me to remember the heat and cold, my father with his teeth knocked to one side by the butt of a rifle, his broken arm and hanging over my left shoulder protecting me, staring straight into the sun, too hurt to die ... my mother begging for water, for life. Guards standing on the tops of the cattle cars urinating on us, on my mother.

Victoria slid from underneath the cover and gently touched his shoulder. "I be right back."

She pulled her wrinkled dress over her head, tiptoed to the door, cautiously peeked out and dashed through the hallway to the toilet a few doors away.

David laced his fingers together behind his head and followed the moving light patterns thrown onto the ceiling from the headlights of cars passing in the street.

Dachau Dachau Dachau Dachau so many lights and so dark

the screams of families being lost and the smell of weakness, hunger, my father being pushed one way, my mother's nose suddenly smashed into her face by a fist, my mother . . . her face changed in a split second . . . my mother . . .

Victoria eased back into the room, dropped her dress in the middle of the floor and felt her way to the kitchen sink for a glass of water.

"David, you want a glass of water?"

"No, no, thanks."

Water water water the dreams of fresh water clear water from streams in the hills around our city. Their city. No Jews allowed. Fresh bread from the oven. No Jews allowed. No bread for Jews. No water for Jews. No air for Jews. No light for Jews. No life for Jews.

She snuggled back into bed, nestled her head under his right armpit.

"You know, you may not think it but I know a little bit about those camps 'n stuff. I remember readin some stuff about how bad them Germans treated y'all."

A tattoo for life licking toilets being degraded bitten by dogs called men. The men called dogs forced to work all day and half the night. Injections with Death less than five seconds; very scientific ovens for people.

"You ain't such a big dude, how did you manage to get through all that stuff?"

"How did I? How did I? How did I? Victoria, please, don't ask me how. I don't know, I just don't know."

Many of the strongest looking ones died first. How strange the strong ones, the soccer players, the athletes, the strong . . .

How did I survive boiled water with blades of grass, bark from the trees, shoe leather, dirt . . . each other . . . anything. The cold wetness and miserable feelings all the time forever.

"David?" Victoria's soft voice echoed from the ceiling . . . and finally one death before Suicide. Suicide. Salvation only hours away and they were gone. Death still a possibility but suicide no longer. Thought about food, warmth, an urge. Never again.

"David?"

He pretended, briefly, to be asleep, taking in the sound of the female voice next to him, moving closer to the voice, loving her woman smell and the softness of the breast against him.

"Day-vid?" He mimicked her way of calling his name and smothered her outraged laughter with a kiss.

If only I could remember what her name was all these years no real feeling until she . . . was she Dutch? Danish? Swedish?

Victoria . . . my dearest Victoria I wonder what my sisters and especially my mother would think to see me in bed with a schwartze, a Gentile . . . small cold silent smile in the dark.

Day-vid? Dayy-vid?

. . .

Mrs. Solomon stirred the tea in her glass absent-mindedly, pushed the tax forms to the upper left hand corner of her desk and slouched in her chair, listening to the sounds of people coming in from work, school, a walk, to check their mailboxes.

So many papers, always papers, forms, papers for this, that, whatever. God! What kind of world would it be without the papers?

She pulled the forms back in front of her with a characteristically deep sigh, took a sip of tea and pushed the papers back again. She sat staring at the wall calendar in front of her for a long minute.

Leo . . . well, how much blood can you get from a turnip?

With a casual motion, as though she had suddenly remembered something, she reached down into her purse leaning against the leg of her chair and pulled her wallet from it.

The picture she eased from the cellophane divider was wrinkled at the edges and yellowed with time. She pushed her glasses back up to the bridge of her nose, propped the photograph against her tea glass and stared at the face in it.

Such a good looking man. But if we do more Nathan I might get pregnant and then we'd have to get married.

Rose, certain things a girl shouldn't do before marriage, the man will lose respect.

Yes, Nathan, I do love you. No, no, Nathan, you didn't hurt . . . you didn't . . .

Oh God such pain for the rest of my life that kind of pain if only I had listened to my mother.

I don't know, Nathan, I don't know yet. I won't know for a few days more.

Well?

We won't have to get married, Nathan.

I would've married you, Rose, you know that, don't you? Write me every day, Rose. A letter every day, agreed?

Yes, yes . . . a letter every day.

The sunshine is unbelievable. We are building a nation under the noses of the British. The foreigners think it's very strange, some of them, for me to be here, a young guy from the Bronx.

My Hebrew is improving. A very difficult, very logical language . . . certain words give me endless problems. How is your mother?

So far away, so far away, we could have been good Jews in the Bronx why did you have to leave me Nathan? We would have been so happy together.

Rose, certain things you shouldn't do before marriage a man will lose respect . . .

Mrs. Solomon removed her glasses and deliberately allowed the tears to blur the picture in front of her before reaching for a tissue.

Rose, for God's sake listen to me, your own mother, for God's sake! You're twenty eight years old already other girls in the neighborhood are bringing home grandchildren. If he were going to send for you by now he would have sent . . . be sensible for God's sake.

But mama I don't love Mr. Solomon and besides he's fifty years old.

Forty eight only.

Well, forty eight only, and he dyes his hair and he's fat and always has bad breath.

Rose, listen to me . . . you *are* my daughter but a great beauty you're not. Be sensible for God's sake, be sensible. Doesn't have such a terrible sound to it, Mrs. Morris H. Solomon.

Good morning Mrs. Solomon, such a nize day.

Good morning Mrs. Gold it is a lovely day.

Rose honey, you're begining to look a little round about the middle. Are you . . . ?

No mama not yet.

Mornin Miz Solomon, you want me to put these groceries over her?

Thank you, Smitty . . . the table is better. Here you are.

Thank you, Miz Solomon, have a good day now.

You too, Smitty. And be sure to tell Herman to save for me a couple good pieces of veal.

Sure will, Miz Solomon.

Rose Rose my God what did you do? Scorch the chicken soup?

Rose Rose you know I like a lot of starch in my collars gives a man dignity to have his neck straight.

Rose Rose you know I love you, don't you?

Rose Rose where's all the money going for God's sake, we have to be careful money doesn't grow on trees you know.

No mama, not yet.

Harry and I will be too old to enjoy our grandkids if . . .

Here lies Morris H. Solomon, a good man. Cardiac arrest, next of kin notified.

Mrs. Solomon replaced her glasses, gently wedged Nathan Cohen's picture back into the cellophane divider and made a wry face as she swallowed the dregs of her cold tea.

With a worried, resigned expression on her face and a deep sigh she returned to her paperwork.

Outrageous these taxes they tax us to death and still can't do anything really worthwhile. Hypocrites!

A large, gothic lettered U.R. at the top left corner of an envelope caught her eye as she worked.

I must clean some of this junk off before it buries me.

She reached across her desk to gather up the stray papers, ripped envelopes, scraps of correspondence, to stack into a neat pile. Office of Urban Renewal.

Wrinkling her brow into a giant question mark, she slowly reached for the letter.

So much junk I can't even get to read my mail.

Dear Owner, we regret to inform you that your structure has been selected for demolishment, in the interests of urban renewal. Reasonable compensation will be granted, after a review of your claim by the Urban Renewal Compensation Board. An appeal must be filed with the Appeals Committee within 90 days . . . if necessary. Sincerely Yours, Mr. Samuel E. Leventhal.

Mrs. Solomon read the letter again, folded it neatly and, as tears streamed down her cheeks, began to tear it into small bits and to tear the small bits into smaller bits.

. . .

Play it again, Sam . . . Talib Dawoud, Brother Yusef, Macmaoud Al Haddi, Sahib Shihab, Ahmal Jamal, Abschlam Ben Schlomo, Rahsaan the Magnificent, Ahmed Abdul Malik,

Sun Ra, Mingus *was* Epithecanthropus Erectus sounds
tonalities atonalities universal mathematics solving the problems we have when nobody's heart beats . . . listen!

Leo took a deep breath, sat up straight, flexed his cramped
fingers and stared at the words he had just written.

Play it again, Sam; something no one ever said or played,
again and again, no names this time no frame of reference
music from wherever the stars maybe or the color red or blue
and most definitely black.

Icicle notes dropped crinkling and tinkling on Kansas City
farmlands New Jersey garbage dumps California manholes
and beaches hoed down cane fields and the Big Sur into and
out of fifteen story huts up and down scribbled up pissy tail
elevators in dingy projects put another nickel in the nickelo-
deon all I want to hear is music/music/music.

Furious firefighter's trucks ambulance sirens Mexican Traffic . . . Cortez used Malinche for his sins sheets of sound
bleep bleep pit lights stop and go Green Yellow Red a giant
metronome skirling 'round corners the meat wagon hit that
note again don't make any quick moves all we got in here
is a dead Bessie Bird-sticks bumped against the ground thump
thump foot-stomped rhythm whistling with hot lips Buddy
Bolden was his name and blowing the horn was his game
thumb and forefinger pop snap crackle and bop shit sho' we
got rhythm ain't everybody?

Indian snakes biting fangs quivering on two small drums
with dancing heads the Sun is what counts and yes I love the
flute as well as the shanai so many beautiful winking grace
notes.

Leo paused, straightened his back again and smiled. And
if It is listening not having to strain Its ears because our hearts
are all pumping in time knowing that Peace, oh well, the
preacher's copout is that It did create us in Its own Image.
In the Beginning was the First Mistake no eraser available

. . . Man-hyphen-It.

And if It ain't listening because there is really nothing to hear and It has been running a Game on us all the time . . .

Time well It should be given responsibility for that too . . .

Time in Time out of Time about Time what Time your Time It's Time Time It!

Leo stuck the ballpoint behind his right ear, eased off his stool as though in a trance, paced slowly around his room, scratched his shorts out of his crotch and remounted the stool.

Time for a woman. Time for three six nine women a pomegranate-nectarine Lady a Lip Lap chick a green woman with duck billed hips, orange eyeballs sky blue eyelashes sliver slit mouth burnt umber breasts mango flavored nipples and a long yellow scream for Love.

A woman . . . a zebra lady with lion fangs elephant joints and cheetah speed. Me a man for this woman a mysterious soulful force a transplanted force d'Afrique negre belle negre negretude orfeu noir le bete noir noir nawwww Now . . . Niggers unite you have nothing to lose but your French!

And after the French is gone and the Romanian and the Prussian and the Finnish and after we have returned to ourselves like the best of the Jews from all over the world Home will once again be in our souls and not soul music and soul sham soul shit soul shock or schlock.

Like the best of the Jews from all over the world like the best of the Jews, not a people or a nation but an idea and a skull cap sweeten the letters of the alphabet fools!

The heat of a blend the end to reason a haiku anapestic in long hand. Please let this be called poetry unless someone takes the time to understand. Really.

Sheer poetry . . . stuff showing through.

Helene was in Greece. No, Mikonos is Greece.

A Dance the Biggest Dance ever held on this world Scotchmen will dance without skivvies Bembe Queen Elizabeth the 99th will dodo in Parliament the Duke will take his hands from behind his back the white man will resurrect the buffalo and forget money. Cochise, Black Kettle, Joseph, Victoria, Crazy Horse, Yellow Hand, Gall, Sitting Bull, Geronimo . . .

Leo slammed his ballpoint down on his writing stand. Awwww shit! this stuff is gettin outta hand! He muttered and hopped off of his stool.

He circled the room twice, slowly, hands clasped behind his back, a frown on his face and plopped, face forward, onto his bed.

He lay there, deliberately smothering himself for a minute and then, unable to bear the thought of no air, rolled over on his back and sucked in deeply.

Gasping, he squinted at the lamplight shining onto the scattered pages on his desk.

He sat up, dangling his feet over the edge of the bed, rocked slightly from side to side.

America . . . Red Folks, Black Folks, White Folks, Yellow Folks, awww what a bunch of tiresome shit!

He stood and stretched himself, walked past the stool and desk, turned back to it, hopped up on the stool and began to write again.

Dreams Dreams I have seen you before I've turned this corner before once or twice dreams.

Minds above at last what might be possible now by any means necessary.

Dreams Dreams Martin had one dreaming men dreamers lurk around the edges learning . . .

And above all after everything is said and done there only remains Life and Death and a few possibilities in between . . . what is Art?

These foolish thangs remind me of you.

He allowed his pen to stir around in midair a few times before placing it in his desk drawer.

He clicked the bent lamp light out and slowly screwed himself around to face the window.

A shooting star flashed across the surface of the window pane, in a split second, a dozen planes collided, fluffy umbrellas ballooned over the collision, searchlights flashed blood red beams against the clouds, white hot shells spiraled from the ground. Is there a Hell? Is there yet a reason for one?

Leo shook his head from side to side, like a rogue elephant, trying to dislodge the huge tear that had frozen itself onto the center of his forehead.

. . .

Samu sprayed Black Flag into the baseboards facing Fred's room, bending closely to his work, stood, caught sight of himself in the mirror on his dresser and impulsively pumped a playful stream of bug killer at his smiling image.   •

Chapter 6

Helena, rolling out from Darius's slender body . . . No!
I will not! her full breasts jiggling gracefully as she swayed
unsteadily to her feet.

"Darius, you are a disgusting man! Disgusting!"

He shuffled himself over onto his back and stared at
Helena's pouting bottom lip, swept a helpless look across the
room at Sire. Sire, sitting up expectantly, alertly, the red tip
of his penis glistening in the foreground of his furred belly.

Darius shrugged, conveying in that gesture a plea for understanding, or indulgence, at least.

Sire turned his head away in disgust and flopped over onto
his side in a corner.

Helena stumbled away from the pallet, eyeing both of them,
suspiciously, mumbled a few Greek gutterals and fled to the
toilet.

Darius watched the toilet door close and turned his face

back urgently, pleadingly, in Sire's direction.

Gutless man . . . can't even get meat . . .

A few minutes later, Helena opened the toilet door, a thoughtful expression on her face, looked out at Sire and, ignoring Darius, called to him in a low alto.

Come here, Sire . . . come here . . . at least you have a hard on.

Sire, sweeping to his feet, paused to shake himself, grinned wolfishly at Darius as he trotted past him onto the toilet with Helena.

. . .

Samu Akintola slyly watched each movement of the lithe, well turned, banana-colored female body standing calmly in front of the window in his room, smoking a cigarette, staring down onto the street. Ooooo my Gawd . . . if only I could just stick the tip in only the tip would . . .

"I had no idea you had such a good view from here, Samu, you can almost see . . . " turning quickly to catch the lascivious look in his eyes and the obscene thoughts stumbling over her body. Male chauvinist asshole . . . I'm just a body, huh? Just another piece of ass, a yellow piece this time . . . hah! We'll see about that.

Samu, slightly embarrassed to be caught looking so lustfully, busied himself about his room, fluffing up the pillows on his sofa, furtively glancing at her full, braless, melon shaped breasts as he did so.

"Angela, would you care for something to drink, a little tot of rom?"

Angela, skeptical eyebrow raised, "that would be nice," she answered, strolling provocatively around his room, pausing to brush her long nailed fingers across the crosswoven loom of the covering on his bed. "Samu, this is beautiful, is it some special kind of cloth?"

Samu, pausing in his haste to pour rum into water glasses. "Oh that, it's called kente."

"It's really beautiful, the design."

"My grandmother gave it to me when I came to America ... to school."

"Really?"

Angela Y. Yang accepted Samu's nervous goodwill offering with a slight, cynical bow and sat gracefully on the sofa, carelessly lotusing her heels across her thighs.

Samu sat at the other end of the sofa, nervously, drink in hand, trying to peer around the corner of Angela's knee and down past her large, firm thighs.

Angela Y. Yang, a studied history, light years away from bound feet, a yellow female with taut thighs, Pa-kua and a noble background from the Middle Kingdom, Macao (damn the Portuguese!) and proud of it, raven haired, smui-e stroked eyes, racially graceful, Asian, by way of the University of Copenhagen, a Moment at the Sorbonne, corridors of the University of Cairo, on to Havana and Fidel, and now the University of Chicago and Afrikan studies.

They sat, slowly sipping, Mandarin and Yoruban, staring at each other over the edges of their glasses, trying to decide who would be responsible for the first move.

. . .

Leo scraped his knuckles back and forth across his forehead, jabbing his forefingers into the eye he felt bleeding in the center of his forehead, the blood, going into his consciousness, from white hot to syrupy warm.

A is for all the Alls in the world for every All that was Anything if All meant if ...

He reread the words backwards, as though he were a beginning reader, three times, four times, slid off his high stool and began walking around the room in a tight circle, a glazed, lost, blank look in his eyes.

. . .

Yes, that's correct . . . Mrs. Rose Solomon!

And we should be grateful for bureaucrats?

Mrs. Solomon slumped over her desk, telephone propped between shoulder and chin, puzzling together the torn up letter from the Department of Urban Renewal.

After five long, dry minutes . . . a voice, metallic, impersonal . . .

Thankk you for holding, Mrs. Lipton's line is clear now.

Mrs. Solomon, jaw muscles flexing with tension, spoke calmly, furiously, coldly.

It is not Lipton I want, it is Leventhal. For the third time to someone I'm saying it, Mr. Samuel E. Leventhal! For God's sake!

Thank you, the metallic voice rang out automatically, one moment pleeessse.

Having successfully puzzled the torn letter together, Mrs. Solomon slumped back heavily in her chair.

Momma always told me I'd end up a hunchback. Rose, if you don't sit up straight you'll make a crook in your back, for God's sake! You'll end up a hunchback! Who wants to marry a hunchback?

She straightened her back and slumped across her desk, stirring her spoon around in her empty tea glass from time to time, determined to sweat it out.

The sound of a rich, mellow baritone pulled her back straight.

Mrs. Solomon?

Yes.

Mrs. Rose Solomon?

Yes.

This is Sam Leventhal.

Oh my God! He sounds like Nathan.

Yes, yes, yes . . . I'm here, Mr. Leventhal. I've been here . . . in her best Yiddish lisp . . . for two tausend years a'ready it seems, waiting.

The baritone chuckled with good humor.

He even laughs the way Nathan used to laugh.

I'm very sorry, Mrs. Solomon, very sorry to have kept you waiting so long; I can really appreciate your patience . . . but, well, you know how it is sometimes, even in the best of well run families there're apt to be little snags, things that happen. At any rate, I apologize for the delay . . . now then, what can I do for you?

Mrs. Solomon's prepared witticism slid from her mind as her bottom lip began to convulsively tremble, and sudden tears blossomed in a soft, full stream on the top of her cheeks.

Tell me please, tell me, Mr. Leventhal . . . why my building? Why must you tear down my building? My whole life . . . Why? Mr. Leventhal? Why?

. . .

"Day-vid? Day-viiddd? Why don't you put that old book down and let's go down to the Flamfloogie Club? I bet you cain't even dance! I'm tired of this room, being hemmed up in here all the time. Dayyy-viidd! Day-vid, when we gon eat some real food? I'm gettin tired of all these knoshes, this creams 'n luxes and . . . "

"Lox, you mean," looking up quickly from *Being and Nothingness*.

Sartre is such a long winded bastard at times, but you have to plow through him to get past the others.

"Yeaaaaah, lox . . . and these old hard ass doughnuts . . . Bagels. What the hell does all this mean? The translator must have been drunk."

Victoria stopped complaining, anxiously pacing around the

room and puffing on her cigarette for a few seconds, took a close look at David's skull-like face peeking calmly over the edge of his book at her.

"You makin fun of me?" With impish, good natured petulance she threw a potato knish at his head.

He stoically blocked the missile with his book and, after piercing Victoria with a long, dirty look, kept on reading.

. . .

Sire spasmed periodically as the memories danced across his brain . . . the little blonde girl squatting to pee pee riding her back her brother who was always tying ropes around his neck strangling him and screaming and stomping and pulling and jerking him around . . .

"C'mon Taffy! C'mon!"

A puppy a two toned ball of liquid fur always being ruffled.

"Oh, how unusual his eyes are, is he blind?"

"No just a mutational thing."

"How quaint . . . "

"C'mon Taffy!" Taffy, the sound of the name they had given him . . . Taffy, made his eyelids flutter, going back: Taffy! Taffy! Taffy! and his family moving to the west coast taking the little blonde girl who let him mount her when she pee peed and sometimes when she didn't pee pee. Moving away out of his eyesight far from his nose. And a strongly muscled brownskinned arm said thatta boy take it easy fella you're a beauty, you won't be in the pound long that's for sure, even if I have to bail you out myself.

. . .

Jeweled fingers pointing imperially a paisley scarf; forty-ish, a dog lover, no little blonde innocent. Knows what she wants why couldn't she have settled for a poodle? They like her type.

206

"That one, that one over there, the wolfish looking one with the odd eyes."

"Oh, that's a good choice, lady . . . only been here a couple days, comes from a good family, too."

Yes, she sees what she sees, she likes it too.

Sire sitting glowing red penis tip unsheathed . . . old bitch!

. . .

Helena followed Sire out of the toilet, scratches on her side from his paws, the stain of his saliva crusted in the crease of her back.

She stood disdainfully over Darius' head, squatted slightly and flushed a stream of urine onto his face as he lay on his pallet crying.

"So, that's what you do, huh? When you meet a real woman, you send her off to fuck your dog! You nutless bastard you!"

She dried between her legs with the hem of her skirt and turned to face Sire, growling fiercely as he stalked across the room.

Shake the dizzy bitch up, show her I can love 'em and leave 'em, especially if they hurt my "master." These are my days, Dog Days.

Helena snatched her purse from a nearby chair, panic showing . . . as she backed toward the door.

"What is this shit? What is this?" She screamed as she flung the door open and ran up the stairs to the first floor.

Sire casually pounced on the door and closed it, paused to nibble viciously at a wandering flea on his hind leg and trotted over to Darius, still sobbing. He sniffed the urine-identification strain from Helena and covered it with his own.

More meat, Darius . . . more meat . . . bring me more meat.

A is not for all the Alls in the world or for every All that meant whatever it was supposed to mean.

A is for definite things, places and people. Armando Peraza, Arruza, Annie Bodden, Aleksandr I. Solzhenitsyn, Arthur Smith, Archie Shepp, Alice Coltrane, Ali Akbar Khan, Aga Khan, Anthony Hamilton, Aretha Franklin, Ali the Awesome, Aunt Bessie, Aunt Mamie, Aunt Mary, Askeland the Generous, As Salaam Alaikum, Albert Ayler, Ama Amadoo, Albert Camus, Achebe, authors, Afrikans, Axum, Afrikan, Afrika, Ashanti, Akan, Afro-Amerikans . . . An Asylum. Adieu . . .

He stared intently at the series of interlocked scrawls on his writing paper and slowly realized that he hadn't clearly spelled a word after . . . if All meant, but had scribbled a stream of A's out that meant exactly what he wanted them to mean, bunched up in places, spread vertically, ignoring all lines, confused, delighting him as he peered beneath the jumble into the Real Meaning.

His nostrils quivering, he scribbled on.

A Human Race the next time, huh? Not a dog eat dog race. Where did all this asshole competition come from anyway?

A Human Race the next time Si! Everybody hitting the tape in nine flat All under three minutes flat. A for Real. A B-ginning.

After the last word he impatiently pushed his ballpoint into the kinks frizzled around his right ear, slid from his perch, wandered aimlessly around the center of the room.

Well, everything Begins and Ends in the Middle anyway, he mumbled and fell onto his lumpy bed.

. . .

I guess this is what she thinks life is supposed to be . . . a too sweet wine, almost sacreligious, homemade bread (homemade bread?) and ... O Father! High Adventure! A few sticks of piss poor marijuana! and television and pedantic conversation and more fucking. What? Again? How many times can she come?

"Freedie?"

"Yes, Joyce?" Sprawling back comfortably on the bosomy Arabian pillows, a potentate, a green dish of melting sherbet on the finely finished ebony coffee table in front of them, passing a crudely rolled joint back and forth.

Shyly, earnestly, an honest supplicant, terrycloth robe opened to show a triangular patch of grizzled hair, rubber shoes, hair washed with beer and egg smile gleaming ... meaningfully.

"Freddie, aren't you sleepy? Both of us will be pretty sleepy tomorrow if we don't get some rest."

Cuddling closer, down to the forefinger and thumb tip burning part of the joint.

The ol' roach clip.

"Joyce, look, I think I ought to be going ... three nights this week we've uhh ... it's eleven o'clock and ... "

Joyce, coyly, fiercely: "Don't you like being with me?"

God, I'm so lonely, so lonely.

. . .

Please believe me, I do understand your position, Mrs. Solomon. I do, believe me ... I do.

How lovely she is. What I guess a lot of the young guys in the office would call ... well preserved. Hell! Who says anyone is old at fifty? Such a sensitive face.

I don't think you do understand my position, Mr. Leventhal. Please, you may call me Rose. This building is my whole life. It isn't just the money I'm concerned about.

Mmmmmm ... such a distinguished looking Jewish man ... comes from a good family I'm sure ... with those hands

209

he could be a surgeon. Something about a man with no hair on top, very intelligent.

Mrs. Solomon, Rose, now you must understand, you must be reasonable. Urban renewal is the best thing for this area. As you know, no doubt, many of the shops are either second rate or out of business, the streets are unsafe after dark, the crime rate is high and rising, most of the buildings in the area are . . . falling apart.

Yes, go on! Say it! Mine is too! Every cent I put back into it for improvements and whatever is left over goes for taxes!

I don't understand them, under the circumstances, why would you want to keep you?

People live in the building, Mr. Leventhal.

Samuel E. Leventhal, urban renewal apologist, public relations man for City Re-planning, sitting alongside Mrs. Solomon's all-purpose desk, leaned over onto the cluttered space, stared at her soulfully and, in a low, rumbling voice . . . dropping his hand across hers interlocked prayerfully.

Rose, if it wasn't for urban renewal there would be no new buildings, no fresh places, if you'll pardon the pun, for people to live in.

She stared at his hand on hers, a neat, well scrubbed man, clean. She moved her eyes up to his and asked softly, "If, in Europe, people can live in old houses, why not here?"

Rose . . . God what an ugly job this can be at times . . . this isn't Europe, this is America, and in America everything is torn down from time to time. What matters is progress, not age.

Mrs. Solomon smiled sarcastically and asked, "Since when is tearing someone's house down considered progress?"

Samuel E. Leventhal, of Urban Renewal, removed his hand from hers and shrugged his shoulders.

Run! Run! Hurry! Run! Run!

Leo popped up in bed, thigh muscles twitching convulsively, face dripping fearful sweat, clamped his hand over his mouth to muffle a scream and looked down at the hand as though it belonged to someone else.

After a long minute he removed his hand and fell back to stare out of the window, the moonlight streaming through the uncurtained window, casting surrealistic shadows down onto Leo's face.

Wonder how Samu got those slashes on his cheeks? Have to ask him about that sometime.

A nigger A made in America Article . . .

The urge to get up and scribble the thought stiffened his body for an indecisive second, but eased away.

A nigger A nigger in America A contradiction in terms An Article of Art Auctioned off Aunt Jemimmed . . .

A cloud passed in front of the moon, pushing his face into murkiness, caused a brief panic to swell up in his throat. The cloud passed on, releasing the moonshine on his face again.

Why am I me? Why here? Which Way is the Way?

That sho was a fine yellow woman I saw Samu with the other day . . . bet he'll act a fool and blow it.

Helena's gone. Long gone. Long may she 'ho. Fred Bruh Freddie the Old Bastard Himself is into Something hope the lady can reveal some thrills on him might do him good at least he wouldn't be so grouchy all the time, maybe.

She said she used to love me said it right across her desk, a tall, slender, pretty faced Modern Black woman minus Current rhetoric, but now she says it was the past and it ain't us no more. O well.

A full moon A full moon moonlight, moonlit moonbright please send me someone to love tonight.

Leo struggled to pull his hands away from his sides, stretch-

211

ing his fingers out like a splayed catcher's mitt and stared at the aura of the moon between them.

Love, have you ever been in love, Leo?

Love what's that money love is that and I ain't got none. No that's not true love ain't money I'm a poet so I oughta know.

He lowered his hands to their former positions, flexing and relaxing his fingers as he did so, surprised to discover that his wrists felt tired from the strain of stretching his fingers.

Hip bone connecte to the thigh bone connected to kneebone kneebone ...

Why can't I love somebody? Why ain't I connected somebody? To anything other than this room, this place. God! Everybody has somebody but me even Mrs. Solomon she sho' is a groovy old broad and even she's got somebody ... bald headed dude wears nice suits too. Who the hell do they think they're fooling old duffers been in and out of the building in and out of Mrs. Solomon's place ten times at least in the last two weeks.

Two male voices having an impatient, high pitched West African argument faded into and out of Leo's hearing range, forced his forehead into a wrinkled frown with the strain of wanting to know what they'd been arguing about. It had to be an argument, folks talking like that.

Think I'll go up to David's. Nawwww, that would be a drag with that silly ass bitch up there with him. Wonder how a dude with as many smarts as David could have let himself get caught in a bind like that? Oh well, who knows what went down? Maybe she's more than she seems to be. Poor David.

Another extension Another dimension Another declension. Hahhh hahhh hahhh hahhah ...

The sound of his laughter, his own voice surprised him and he abruptly stopped, lured back into himself by his wandering mind.

Darius must've scared Helena shitless ... and left me bitchless, with his dirty rotten dog.

Wonder what him and that old freaky lookin dog of his did, to chase a cold blooded 'ho like Helena back out into the world Me-kannos! Mykonos! Uhh huh ...

Darius! Devil in His Hell!

Dealing with God in His Heaven!

Damn wish I had some good smoke.

He laboriously twisted over onto his side and stared at the stark outline of his writing table, the high stool in front of it and the collapsible lamp curled, snakishly, over his pages.

Did I turn off the light before I laid down or has it been off all the time? Have I been writing in the dark? Who turned off the light? Did I turn off the light? Leo squeezed his eyes shut for ten seconds, mumbling the count and quickly opened them, shocked to see the desk light gleaming brightly at him.

After a disoriented minute he realized that the bright illusion was the result of his imagination and reflected moonlight.

The light is off doesn't matter who turned it off or how it got turned off nobody wants to see me anyway.

Two large tears burbled out of the corners of his eyes.

Nobody wants to see me anyway why should they? So I can write a poem about them who wants a poem written about them or for them? I wish I was God I would make everybody need a poem.

Well, Mrs. Hunter, we find your son to be ... uh, somewhat, well, unusual. But, of course, in time, with proper treatment, he could ... uhh ...

Leo? Leo? What in the world are you doin, boy! With your hand down there in that toilet stool?

Wanna find out where it goes, momma.

The tears ran faster, across the bridge of Leo's nose, dripping onto his dirt splotched sheets.

What's wrong, cousin Leo? You don't like it down here or

something?

Why you so quiet, son?

Mu'deah! mu'deah! I saw Leo stickin his thang inna waddamelon!

Now lissen here, Leo. We promised yo momma, 'fore she passed, bless her sweet soul, that we would take care of you, you being my nephew 'n all, but you really makin thangs hard for everybody.

What am I doin, Uncle Willie?

Josie told Mu'deah she saw you stickin yo pee pee into a hole you plugged in a wadamelon.

What's wrong with that, Uncle Willie?

. . .

Victoria leaned against the door frame, a brush, a natural comb, rope soled sandals, three peasant skirts and a scroll of her astrological chart stuffed into her open mesh bag.

"I'm goin, David. David? I said . . . "

"I heard you, Victoria. Goodbye."

God please leave don't make it ugly it's been so beautiful the most beautiful time. Even the stupid parts have been beautiful, let's just be incompatible, not ugly. Please.

"Well? Ain't you gon say nothin else? Or are you just gon-na sit up there with that lil old funny lookin beanie stuck on the back of your head'n stare at me like I'm crazy or somethin?"

David glared into Victoria's face, both of his eyes squeezed into murderous slits.

"Get out of here," he said softly, viciously.

"You don't have to be so mean and nasty about it! I was just joking about your lil old—"

"Get out of here before I kill you!"

Victoria struck another pose, placing one hand on her hip and flexed her left leg provocatively, took a close look at the

214

mailicious brightness in David's eyes and thought better of making a protest.

David wrenched the door open behind her.

"Get out now!"

She slunk past him, avoiding his eyes and, a few paces down the hall, turned, sadly.

"I didn't know you was so sensitive."

He slammed the door shut, tears clouding his vision.

Why is love so dangerous for me?

. . .

Yes, Sam, you're right. Of course you're right, I wouldn't be concerned, worried, bothered by any of it if I didn't have it but . . .

No buts! Here . . . sign the papers, Rose. What sense wouuld it make to have such a problem on your shoulders?

She looked down at the half folded documents on her desk, frowned her brow at the X marked line and up into Samuel E. Leventhal's face.

Yes, Rose. It *is* the best thing. There's no way for this place to be left standing, not with the whole block half gone already.

She sat heavily at her desk, took the pen from his hand and signed four copies of an agreement in weak, scraggly strokes.

What will I tell them, Sam? What will I . . . ?

Tell them the truth, Rose . . . tell them the truth, you just couldn't beat City Hall.

He folded the pages neatly, stuffed them into a long, brown envelope and punched it down inside the breast pocket of his suit.

Now then, enough for business.

Hah! Easy for you to say, the business is just beginning for me.

Fred, Samu, David, my poor Davidka, Leo, Darius, even

215

Darius and that animal of his . . . and all the others.

Samuel Leventhal bent in a courtly manner and tapped Rose Solomon gently on the forearm, bringing her back.

Rose, I know this may sound out of line and if you should think so, I ask your forgiveness.

Nathan Nathan Nathan . . . so long ago, forgive me.

I know our relationship, thus far, has been . . . uh . . . strictly business, strictly.

Rose Solomon's chin line softened, her eyes took on a girlish gleam as she looked up coyly at Samuel Leventhal's glistening forehead.

Yes, Sam?

Well, I was wondering . . . would it be possible for you to forget that I am Mr. Samuel E. Leventhal from the office of Urban Renewal? And simply think of me as just plain Sam Leventhal, widower, a guy for whom you don't have extraordinary fondness, I couldn't ask you if you'd like to have dinner with me at Gordon's Restaurant this evening. But, as "just plain Sam," I could.

She unsuccessfully tried to muffle the sudden smile that pushed dimples into both corners of her mouth.

Well, will you, Rose? I really hate to eat alone . . .

She nervously shuffled a pile of papers from one corner of her desk to another corner, opened and peeked into her desk drawer as though looking for something.

He gently grabbed her wrist.

Will you, Rose? The strudel is fantastic.

She shook her head to indicate no, no, no, but answered yes, yes, yes.

Just plain Sam, a delighted grin on well fitted dentures.

Fine! That's really fine! Listen, I have to run by the office to clear up a couple things, rush home to shave . . . pick you up at 7:30?

She shrugged, a hopeless shrug; it's been such a long time

216

since I've been out with a man. How does one act?

Sam Leventhal, easing out, beaming, took a last look before closing the door.

It's been a long time for me too, Rose. Remember that, for me too, Rose.

She straightened her back, coquettishly touched the bun in back of her head and smiled at how cleverly he had read her thoughts.

7:30. I'll be ready, Sam, I'll be ready.

. . .

"Tell me, Samu, do you give me, any woman, credit for having any intelligence?"

Samu, bracing himself on his elbow beside Angela, head resting in the palm of his hand.

"What? What are you talking about? I don't understand—"

Angela turned toward him, cold fury flicking from her slanted eyes. "You know damned well what I'm talking about!"

Beads of perspiration popped out on his forehead, frowns screwed his face into a dark, puzzled knot. Angela flipped the wrinkled sheet off of their naked bodies, strode over to the dresser for her cigarettes.

Samu pulled the sheet back up over his hips, tucked his swelling penis between his legs, watching the dappled sunlight pour through the wrinkles and pin pricks of the drawn shade.

She lit a cigarette, leaned against the dresser and folded her arms, staring at Samu's moist forehead and his flaring nostrils.

"You're just like all the rest!"

Samu sat up in bed quickly, lost control of his hardened penis which tentpoled the sheet.

"I don't understand you, Angela . . . I just don't . . . "

217

She smirked at him, strolled over to the window, rolled the beaten shade up and stood. Gloriously, for a moment, her yellow body shimmered in the deep gold of the evening sunlight.

She turned from the window to sit at the opposite end of the bed, legs folded up in a full lotus position, taking Samu's breath away.

"I thought you might be different," she spoke as though in a trance.

"I thought you might be different. An African, an Asian, an alliance between, some hope for a different kind of relationship! But no! Nothing doing! No way, baby! Same old dreary story. I walk in, you put it in and when you're finished you pull it out, wipe it off and get ready for the next time."

Samu sucked his cheeks in angrily.

"Yes, it's true, don't look so goddamned surprised! We've been fucking for almost a month. Yes, that's right! I called it fucking! What do you call it?"

"Angela! Angela!" Samu, excited, shaking his forefinger in her direction, "let me tell you something!"

"No! Dammit! Let me finish . . . in all this time you've never even asked me whether I had come or not, never given any consideration for any pleasure but your own."

He felt his developing argument fade, his engorged penis quietly grow limp between his legs as he leaned back against the bars of the bedstead to listen to Angela's tirade against unfeeling, insensitive males, like himself.

"That's one of the reasons why this country is so fucked up today, it's because of millions of inconsiderate bastards like you who don't care, don't care about anything beyond whether or not they've busted their fuckin nuts!"

I'll wait 'til she finishes. Wait until she's blown off all the steam she needs to blow off. Thank God African women

218

haven't gotten on this lib stuff completely.

. . .

Mrs. Solomon leaned back against the fake leather uphol-
stery in their booth, covering her mouth politely as she
burped, her cheeks flushed with two glasses of the house wine
and the excitement of Samuel E. Leventhal's attentive
presence.

Sooo, after my wife died, uhh, passed on . . .

. . .

Sire carried his harness and leash to Darius and dropped
them in front of him, indicated that he wanted to have it put
on and taken for a walk.

Darius stared at the harness and into Sire's eyes.

Sire stared back, forcing Darius to drop his eyes and hook
the harness and leash on him.

Darius' hands shook, trying to snap the hooking parts
together.

Sire growled at his clumsiness.

. . .

**To All Tenants: It is with profound regret that I must
inform you that Urban Renewal has claimed my building
and that I must request that you vacate your rooms by
the end of the month (June 30).**

**Overdue rent *must* be paid before the end of the month.
Very regretfully, Mrs. Rose Solomon.**

. . .

"Fred, I've always loved you, you knew it from the beginning."

Fred sipped his coffee and flashed a benign smile in Joyce's
direction.

"Coffee isn't bad, at least not as bad as it was yesterday."

"I used to watch you stride in every morning, every morning but Monday ... they both smiled ... on every morning except Monday you strode in, looking around at the people in the office as though they were worms."

"Including you?"

Joyce, brushing a few wisps of hair back from her forehead ...

"I think you looked at me as though I were the biggest worm of all."

"Really?"

"Especially after that party ... "

Fred, kindly: "You weren't a virgin, which really, well, to be frank with you, surprised me."

Joyce shook her head shyly, as though trying to ward off the implications she felt in the statement.

"There were only two other men before you, before the party. And," she playfully punched him on the shoulder, causing his cup to rattle in his saucer, "you had me making a fool of myself about you. Remember that afternoon we had lunch at Gordon's?"

"Ummm huh, how could I ever forget?"

"I knew then, despite the fact that you let me make an ass of myself, that you felt something for me."

Fred carefully placed his cup and saucer on the coffee table, kicked the house slippers that she had given him, with pom poms, off, and, with an expression of mock lust on his face, crawled over to Joyce splayed out of the opposite end of the sofa.

"You're right, woman! Absolutely right! What I really wanted was your body!"

She squirmed around under his tickling fingers, not really trying to escape, as he unfastened the belt of her terrycloth robe and blew on her navel, his cheeks distended with the effort, tickling her into spasms of girlish laughter.

. . .

David took a few steps away from his bookcase, a book in each hand, to a large cardboard box, carefully packed the books in beside the others, stared at the tattoo on his forearm and, ant-like, continued the process.

Another move, another place this time, not a camp but still another place . . . why not Israel?

The thought jarred him to a stop. Everyting seemed to stop. Yes, why not Israel?

. . .

Leo pushed his window up as though performing a ritual, grasped the ledge with both hands as he leaned out to look down onto the small hours of the morning.

The hint of a true dawn glowed on his face. He looked back over his right shoulder at the light shining over his desk.

No need for light now.

He straightened up suddenly, bumping his head on the raised window, ignored the brief, sharp pain and walked over to click his light off. No need for light now.

Back at the window he turned to look back over his shoulder, a puzzled look on his face.

Who turned the light off? O well, fuck it! It doesn't matter now anyway. Who needs light?

The early morning chill goose pimpled his arms as he climbed up on the window ledge, to sit with his body poised on the outer edge of the ledge, his feet dangling in midair.

Something's wrong. Ain't that a bitch! Something *is* wrong.

He twisted himself around, carefully placing one foot after another on the floor.

In a cool, detached fashion he unbuttoned his shirt, stripped his undershirt off, shoes and sox, pants and shorts and

221

smiled toward the open window as though it were a mirror.

On the ledge again, facing out onto space and the wire mesh fence three floors between his heels. He leaned, swayed back and forth on the ledge, the strain of trying not to hold onto the ledge hurting his wrists.

Dead Death High no longer Black but Dead. A Dead Black. Everyone needs to die sometimes. If only I could sell a few deaths. A poet seeking employment as an echo an echo an echo . . .

A piece of paper a piece of paper . . .

He reached behind his ear, delighted to find his ballpoint still behind his right ear, and with his left hand reached down to pick up the piece of paper he saw on the ground.

Awwww shit!

He became aware, rationally, soberly, that he was tumbling over and over, that he was flying.

Like a bird, silently. Like a naked butterfly, no fluttering wings only arms. No music but the quick morning wind swhoosing past his ears. Am I screaming?

No screams locked up excited an they've always tried to make me believe it was painful ain't nothin to it a baby could do it.

God, I'm falling, falling, falling . . . no practice for this . . . this thisness.

The fence . . . the fence is coming at me gotta dodge can't dodge who the hell stuck this fuckin thing up here anyway where's that piece of paper I saw?

God, I wish I had been better at what I did while I was alive . . . ooooo sloooowwwww I goooooo.

It's just down there a lil bit a lil bit more.

Through space in space on space their space our space my space spaced out. Everything should be Everything.

Atoms of bursting lights slammed through Leo's skull as he hit the fence, crumpled off of it like a rag doll and blooped